THE STONE WĒTĀ

OCTAVIA CADE

This novel is entirely a work of fiction. The names, characters and incidents portrayed in it are the work of the author's imagination. Any resemblance to actual persons, living or dead, events or localities is entirely coincidental.

Paper Road Press
www.paperroadpress.co.nz

Published by Paper Road Press 2020

Copyright © Octavia Cade 2020
Octavia Cade asserts the moral right to be identified as the author of this work.

A catalogue record for this book is available from National Library of New Zealand Te Puna Mātauranga o Aotearoa.

ISBN 978-0-9951355-0-5

All rights reserved. Apart from any fair dealing for the purpose of private study, research, criticism or review, as permitted under the Copyright Act, no part may be reproduced by any process without the permission of the publisher.

THE STONE WĒTĀ

OCTAVIA CADE

PAPER ROAD PRESS

THE STONE WĒTĀ

Hemideina maori
In winter, the mountain stone wētā crawls into crevices, into cracks in the stone, and it squats there waiting. It is a creature of summer days and winter strengths, of cryogenic hibernation. When the world freezes around it, becoming a stretch of snow and ice and darkness, the stone wētā freezes solid in its bolthole. Over eighty percent of the water in its body turns to ice. The wētā is climate in a single body. It is a continent broken off, geology made flesh.

When the weather warms, the wētā thaws and resumes its life amidst the stone monuments of the Rock and Pillar range.

#

Female wētā survived the cold more readily than the males. The Stone Wētā laughed under her breath. There was a frigidity joke to be made there somewhere, but in her experience winter was a time to lie low and endure and women were better at that, overall, than men. Resistance was revolution, sometimes, blood and dramatic acts, but more often it was survival. More often it was preservation, and the data she carried with her was for preservation more than revolution.

The new data she'd received, smuggled over from Resurrection in a tiny drive, hung down between new breasts. The Stone Wētā was still getting used to the weight of them, in love with the curves of the body she'd always felt she was meant to have. The university had been supportive of her transition, colleagues coming by with easy-freezing foods so she wouldn't have to cook so soon out of the hospital, and there was still some leave left. But the Stone Wētā didn't like to stash data where it might be searched for, or where someone could stumble over it when they popped by to fill up her cupboards.

"There's such a thing as too dedicated," said her doctor when the Stone Wētā decided to go back to work early. The invertebrates could wait, he argued, but what he didn't know was that they were only an excuse. The Stone Wētā had an insulated lockbox hidden up in the Rock and Pillars, buried deep in a lonely crevice.

The lockbox was stuffed with climate data. Information from another country, an administration that was purging files. The Stone Wētā was a biologist with colleagues in other disciplines, and she kept their geology for them.

#

Selaginella lepidophylla
A desert dweller, the resurrection plant is adapted to dehydration, to the long dry seasons of its arid environment.

When parched for short periods, its outer stems curl into circles, but as the waterless days endure the resurrection plant hunches further down, its inner stems compressing into spirals and minimising surface area. Tucked in, the resurrection plant survives almost complete desiccation. Until the rains come it takes on the appearance of a dead thing, but beneath the surface there is revival waiting.

#

Resurrection was raised on the southern borders of the Chihuahuan Desert. She played there as a child – carefully at first, until she learned to adapt her play to climate – and she was grateful for that apprenticeship in aridity. It had taught her what it was to have boundaries, and what it was to have them broached. Water evaporated out in the desert, sweated through skin that seemed sometimes to be a too-permeable thing.

But then all borders were permeable. There wasn't a wall built that couldn't be overcome, and although Resurrection had relatives she no longer saw, could no longer see for they were afraid of leaving a country they might not be able to return to, she had other means of contact.

A botanist was expected to attend conferences, to promote the conservation of her region. "Mexico has one of the most biologically diverse deserts on the planet," she said, talking of the work she was doing, the population surveys, the challenges of long-term monitoring. "We have a responsibility to ensure the preservation of this natural wonder." She took some of the attendees on a field trip, introduced them to ecologies not their own.

In the middle of the hike, one of the foreign scientists – a woman who was deliberately, inanely chatty in her conversation and as such roundly ignored by the rest of the party – stumbled in the sand. When Resurrection took her hand to help her up, a drive was pressed into her palm.

"Thanks," said the scientist. "Clumsy me! Always tripping over my own feet."

"You're welcome," said Resurrection, pocketing what was given to her without a glance. "But it wasn't your feet you tripped over. Have you seen this plant?" She explained about the curling as the others gathered round, demonstrated the beginnings of reversal with her water bottle. "It's amazing what can survive out here," she said.

For all the drama of above-ground, of the resurrection leaves, it was what was buried beneath that she found most important.

Root systems went deep in the desert.

#

The Stone Wētā always copied any data she was given before she buried it in the Rock and Pillars. Caching data was a useful fall-back, but caches had been discovered before. The Stone Wētā had only heard bits and fragments, passed on from her own minimal sources, but Bristlecone Pine had gone silent. Arrested, most likely, with her data confiscated and, presumably, destroyed.

The risk of similar destruction was why data was spread internationally now, each piece of information replicated and hidden at several sites. The Stone Wētā didn't know all of them.

She only knew who she was to pass her data sets on to. That way her potential for betrayal was limited.

"Not that I would, not if I had any choice," she promised. She tried very hard not to think of the choices that Bristlecone might have been given. (The choices that might have been taken away.)

"We all like to think that we'd be brave," said the Glass Sponge. She'd come to stay for the party the Stone Wētā was throwing, to celebrate her new shape with friends while she could. "A Show-Us-Your-Tits Party," she continued, into her third wine and tactful with it.

"You're all class," said the Stone Wētā, emptying the bottle. "Such a fucking lady. And you should be so lucky."

The Glass Sponge sighed, wistful, and the Stone Wētā sniggered into her glass. She'd been recruited by the other woman a couple of years previously. They'd flatted together at uni, and the Stone Wētā hadn't ceased to be amazed that such were the things resistance was made of – the memories of Dunedin winter, cheese rolls and tramping; a history of shared homework and early morning lectures. Soft power and social circles.

"My turn to find someone soon," she said.

#

Scolymastra joubini
The glass sponge crouches on sea beds beneath the Antarctic ice. The silica skeleton sways in the dark water, chilled by the currents of a continent. It is the oldest organism on the planet; for 15,000 years, perhaps, the glass sponge has endured a long

night, its growth a slow and silent thing. But the ice shelves collapsing above have brought light and plankton in levels the glass sponge is not accustomed to. It grows wildly, branching out quickly, while destruction takes place above it.

#

The Glass Sponge spent her summers in the Antarctic, trying to determine the effects of a shifting climate upon polar biota. She was part of a community there: scientists stacked on top of each other, a small society isolated by climate and vocation.

Her secondary role was an open secret. Scott Base was a facility set up for knowledge and the sharing of it, run by a country that was far enough away from the seats of power that it was frequently overlooked. Being small and hidden away at the bottom of the world had its uses, and unimportance was as much a defence as armour.

"Don't you ever want to just come straight out with it?" the Glass Sponge was asked. "Say to hell with it, Scott Base will take your data, send copies to us and we'll store it away where no-one can tamper with it."

"I'm sure the government would love that," she said.

"It's not like New Zealand hasn't told a superpower to fuck off before. We did it on nukes, we can probably get away with it on climate. It might encourage those bastards in Wellington to finally take a stand for once."

"If Wellington wants to come out on data protection I won't stop them," said the Glass Sponge. "But I'm not in charge of what we do here, and I'm not just talking about the Base. I didn't set up this network. The person who did is responsible for scientists all around the world – and not all of them live in countries that wouldn't sell them out if power came knocking."

There was no answer to that. The Glass Sponge waited to be asked who *was* in charge, but the question never came. She took that discretion for the support that it was and was grateful.

Besides, even if she were aware of the real-world identity of the Sand Cat she would never have shared it. Some secrets weren't hers to tell.

#

Felis margarita
The sand cat protects itself from sunlight, and from the lack of it. The desert is a place of extreme temperatures and the bottom of the sand cat's feet, the spaces between its toes, are thick with fur for when the sand is scalding in the noon sun. This fur blurs its footsteps, and the tracks of the sand cat through the dunes are hard to follow.

The sand cat, relative to its size, bites harder than any other feline.

#

The Sand Cat learned early and well the importance of preservation, and of libraries. The Timbuktu manuscripts were the pride of her city, hundreds of thousands of them spread through numerous private households. As a girl, the Sand Cat had seen her uncle inherit the family library, had seen him swear to protect it for the whole of his life, as was right and good.

As a woman, the Sand Cat had seen those manuscripts to be a source of danger as well as pride. The Islamic fundamentalists in northern Mali had tried to destroy them, and while they had managed to burn some, the people of Timbuktu had come together to preserve the rest. Manuscripts were bundled up, buried, smuggled out of the city to safety, a costly and perilous process but one that had resistance and love of learning down its very spine. Residents endangered themselves, endangered their families, by accepting small parcels of texts to hide in their homes. People were beaten every day on the streets for lesser crimes. They were mutilated, they were executed.

They hid the manuscripts regardless.

When the Sand Cat saw the same thing happening again, albeit in other countries and with other targets, perpetrated this time by governments instead of rebels, she refused to countenance it.

The very idea offended her. It offended her down to the marrow, and the Sand Cat felt herself begin to hiss with rage.

"Why do they keep trying to do this?" she spat. "It is knowledge they go after every time!"

"Of course it is," said her uncle. "People who know nothing can be controlled." His texts had been saved, but the effort had turned his hair to iron.

"It has done the same to my heart," said the Sand Cat.

Timbuktu had taught her the value of knowledge, and of preservation. It had also taught her how to network. The Sand Cat was involved in setting up reforestation projects, working to increase planting, and this gave her access to scientists involved in similar projects in other countries. It was perfectly acceptable for her to consult with them on best practice, on their strategies for environmental conservation and how best to involve affected communities. Such consultation was not only normal, it was encouraged.

And if the conversation wandered, what of it?

#

Geckolepis megalepis
The fish-scale gecko is an escape artist of particular and gruesome aspect. Its sister-species amputate themselves in the face of predation, but the fish-scale gecko holds its escape in its skin instead of its tail. That skin is large-plated and scaly, and its attachment to the flesh beneath is temporary. When the fish-scale gecko is grabbed or threatened, it sheds its skin and skitters, bald and pulsing, into the trees.

#

The Fish-scale Gecko was in constant contact with the Sand Cat. Madagascar was not Mali, but the Fish-scale Gecko spent her days as a park ranger, encouraging eco-tourism in the tropical forests. "Poverty is a trap," she said. "People need to live. And if slash-and-burn is the only way for them to make a living, then that's what they'll do. You have to find a way to make sustainable use of the forests economically viable."

The Sand Cat knew that, but she made appropriate noises anyway, and was seen to take notes. Escape was a useful survival tactic but camouflage was better. "Eco-tourism is proving a viable option, then?" she said.

"Over 50% of visitors take part in some form of eco-tourism. The forests are a big part of that. Something I've found tourists particularly enjoy is being hoisted up into the tree tops. It gives them a whole new perspective on rainforest ecology. That's particularly useful given how much tropical forest cover is decreasing globally."

Other operatives might hide the data entrusted to them in the ground, but the Fish-scale Gecko was a creature of heights and canopies, and when she stashed it was arboreal.

"Is this just at the one location?" asked the Sand Cat.

"For now, but it's a popular activity. Too popular, perhaps. I begin to think all the activity in one area is compromising the local ecology."

Over the monitor, the Sand Cat froze. It was almost imperceptible, had not the Fish-scale Gecko been looking for it. "That is . . . concerning."

"I've been scouting for new sites. But we've a busy programme of local events coming up, so I might have to put it off for a little while."

"You've been so helpful," said the Sand Cat. "I really appreciate the time you've spent advising me. I realise I've been adding to your workload. Would it be useful to put our consultations on hold for a few months?"

"That's probably a good idea," said the Fish-scale Gecko. Her skin itched, and she could feel the talons closing around.

#

"We're going to miss you."

"I've still got a few months," said the Stone Wētā. "But thank you. I'll miss you too. I'll miss everyone here. The department's been good to me, and that's in no small measure down to the administration. Down to you."

"My pleasure," said her department head. "You've been a real boon to us. It's not many universities can say that one of theirs has been tapped for Mars."

"Mars needs entomologists too!" said the Stone Wētā. The first manned mission, a colony of scientists – and that mission one-way. "It's an extraordinary opportunity, to help create an ecosystem."

"You've certainly had practice," said the head. Her voice was carefully bland. "I mean, of course, your work up in the Rock and Pillars. Though I suppose that's as much preservation as creation."

"It's an extraordinary interaction between organism and environment," said the Stone Wētā. "It deserves to be protected."

"Absolutely. Oh, talking of the extraordinary, you won't believe what's turned up in my inbox. Accusations that someone at this university is *smuggling*, if you can believe it. Smuggling data. Ridiculous – sounds like they're fishing to me. I forwarded the email on to Foreign Affairs, told them I didn't know anything about it."

"Don't you?" said the Stone Wētā, her voice level.

"Not a thing," said the head. Her gaze was very direct. "And I certainly don't have time to go looking. I'm too busy hunting for a replacement for you!"

"I'm sorry to cause you trouble," said the Stone Wētā.

"If you're that sorry you can help out. There's a young woman visiting next week, come for an interview. She's a potential grad student, looking to do her PhD. Was recommended by a colleague over in Suva – she did some summer fieldwork there in her undergrad. I'd like you to talk with her, see what you think. I hear she's very independent-minded. I like that in this department."

"I've noticed," said the Stone Wētā.

#

Asterias amurensis
The Japanese sea star owes its success to adaptability and reproductive strategy. It owes that success, as well, to the interconnection of the world. Its larvae, spread through ballast waters, are shipped to other oceans and other countries. It is one of the most invasive species alive, and there is hungry persistence in each of its five arms.

#

One of the things that the Japanese Sea Star enjoyed most about marine biology was that it gave her the opportunity, so often, to speak with others in her field. The marine environment was linked, all of it flowing together, and the conferences were frequently global in subject as well as in participants.

She had just attended a particularly interesting session on the effects of climate change upon Antarctic glass sponges. Her own contribution, as one of a panel on combating invasive species, was scheduled for later that afternoon. It promised to be popular – invasion was an issue that could exercise many a biologist.

"We so often have to deal with pests. It's rewarding to find a way to hit back! A job for scientists of sneakiness and strategy." She grinned coquettishly as she said it, circulating through the morning tea, relishing responses. The Japanese Sea Star was aware that she looked pretty and small and unthreatening. Charm was her greatest asset.

"I need a deputy who can make connections quickly," the Sand Cat had told her. "Someone who can accurately and discreetly assess the character of others. Someone people will trust."

"I'm your woman," the Japanese Sea Star had said. "I've a very long reach. Fingers everywhere!" And held them up, wriggling. Her nails were brightly painted.

It amused her to take the name of an invasive to fight invasion. She'd seen what happened when things went wrong. It wasn't enough to store data online, to spread it over the net where everyone could see it. Viruses could change that data easily enough, falsify findings and make the effects look smaller than they were, make the data less of a threat – and without a hard copy to compare it to, without the original data cached, it was difficult to prove the tampering.

The Japanese Sea Star didn't hold a cache. Instead she held drives in her bright pretty handbag, and handed them out like candy at conferences, albeit quietly and carefully. A good proportion of the scientists attending worked for her anyway, and the contents of their own handbags would later disgorge in other waters, and go to ground in foreign shores.

#

"I've felt a chrysalis for so long," said the Stone Wētā. "Transformation comes easily to me." Change of body, change of purpose. Change of planet. "Well, not always easily. But it comes and I have learned to adapt to that. It doesn't work that way for everyone."

"If you think I don't understand necessity and change you can think again," said the girl. The girl – she wasn't very much younger than the Stone Wētā. And she had a name, but the Stone Wētā tried not to think of it. That name was irrelevant – she was here to see if there was a Fish-eating Spider, not a tired young woman from Tuvalu, forced into immigration as a child because of rising waters.

"Why *Dolomedes dondalei*?" asked the Stone Wētā.

The girl who might be the Fish-eating Spider shrugged. "There aren't many species where individuals go hunting for prey bigger than they are," she said. "I found it refreshing."

"You're angry."

"My home is being swallowed up by climate. No-one gives a shit. You think my family was the last to leave? Hell, we weren't even the first. We left years ago. I can't even speak the language anymore! How's that for transformation?

"No-one gives a shit," she said again. "It's all screwing with data now, trying to pretend that nothing's happening. Fine. We're all going to pretend everything's *fine*. I can pretend too. But I'm going to pretend with an insect I can at least admire for gumption, because God knows the people around me don't have any."

"It's a dangerous identification though, isn't it?" said the Stone Wētā, remembering the sound of ancient trees gone quiet, of the silence where Bristlecone Pine had been. She couldn't let anyone else get involved without making sure that they knew the risks they were taking. "Identification like that might make it easy to forget that hunting generally goes the other way."

The girl narrowed her eyes, and for an instant the Stone Wētā could see in them the shadow of many legs. "Sometimes danger is necessary," she said.

#

Dendrocnide moroides
The gympie gympie covers itself with stinging hairs and neurotoxin. It is one of the most poisonous plants in the world, and one of the most painful. A human who brushes up against a gympie gympie will experience agony for up to two years: a persistent reminder of trespass.

It flourishes best after disturbance, when the ground is overturned and in full sunlight.

#

The Gympie Gympie buried her caches in shallow soil. She didn't use a single lockbox, didn't add to the same location more than once. Instead there were a dozen little burials, all in the open air with gaps in the rainforest canopy above. Atop each burial she planted a small specimen of *D. moroides*.

She wore protective gear when she planted; amused herself by picturing what would happen if some poor bastard came looking for what he shouldn't. The Gympie Gympie's ancestors had walked the tropical ecosystems of northern Australia for tens of thousands of years before the Europeans came, and she had been raised with their knowledge, had gone away to university for ecology and come home to her own lands.

She didn't much care if she were followed; there were more dangers here than interrogation, than imprisonment and the betrayal of science. No-one that followed would know those dangers like she did. Anyone alien enough, who didn't know what they were getting into, deserved what they got as far as the Gympie Gympie was concerned. There was a reason she supplemented the buried seeds of science with silica and poison, and it was so the lands of her childhood weren't ravaged further than they had to be when the climate turned.

The Sand Cat might have prioritised preservation, but the Gympie Gympie was all about justice. Her own country wasn't so fucking innocent, and she had no pity left in her burials for guilt.

#

Buellia frigida
This Antarctic lichen of the Dry Valleys grows slowly, perhaps a single centimetre for every millennium, but it does grow. The lichen is so accustomed to extreme cold and aridity that it is used as an approximation of what life may be capable of on Mars. Experiments on the International Space Station, where the lichen is exposed to the conditions of space, as well as to a

simulation of Martian environments, prove that the lichen is capable of enduring both.

#

The Antarctic Lichen floated through the ISS, making her way to the docking port. The transports to the Mars colony were almost ready to go, and the scientists who had been ferried up and through the ISS to their respective ships had almost been offloaded. Only a few were left, and the Antarctic Lichen, assigned on permanent rotation to the Station, was going to say goodbye.

She didn't know the Stone Wētā, had never been informed of her true name, but when the Stone Wētā had first stepped aboard with the tattoo curling round her forearm, all spiky legs and long antennae and big, striped body, the Antarctic Lichen had recognised her.

"Nice ink," she said.

"Kind of a last-minute reminder," said the Stone Wētā, smirking. "I'm still not entirely sure of what. Endurance, maybe."

"Persistence," said the Antarctic Lichen. "Rebirth, into a different world." The world below them hung in space, green and blue and with the ice at its edges draining, the polar caps melting away almost as she watched.

"Transformation," said the Stone Wētā. "I am . . . familiar with the concept."

There was little chance to talk. But as the Stone Wētā prepared to disembark, the Antarctic Lichen gave her a small box. "If you could transport that over to your ship I'd be grateful," she said. "Last minute additions for *Buellia*. Just pass them on, please."

Anyone around them would have thought the box was to be handed over to the colony's botanical department. *B. frigida* was making the trip and it gave the Antarctic Lichen some comfort to know, after all her experiments on it, that if the lichen's native environment were at risk then there was, still, the potential for it to survive on other worlds.

Mars had the potential to preserve a lot.

"It's amazing what can survive in such inhospitable places," said the Stone Wētā.

"I have every faith," said the Antarctic Lichen, waving through the window in the airlock. It was perhaps paranoia that made her send data to the open plains of another planet, but she couldn't keep hoarding on the ISS, where there were limited opportunities to unload.

Data that couldn't be shared was always at risk.

#

The Fish-eating Spider stared up into the dark. Though she could not see it, the ship carrying the Stone Wētā had begun its journey to a harder planet. The Fish-eating Spider did not envy her. She would have missed the stream-sides, the night-sounds of water and the creatures that lived beside it. The way the earth smelled when she turned it over for burial, the shovel new-bought and shiny in her pack.

A drive of smuggled data hung between her breasts, waiting for the morning.

THE ANTARCTIC LICHEN

Variation within a species is a potential advantage for the survival of that species under changing environmental conditions. Such variation in the Antarctic lichen can be limited, and sampled populations show low levels of genetic diversity. There is, however, some indication that glacial refugia exist and that those refugia populations may exhibit some private alleles.

#

The Antarctic Lichen was used to a very specific sort of isolation: one that came with company of a sort much like herself. And she enjoyed the company of other scientists, she did, but there were times in her career she felt herself yearning for a little more variety. Something a bit less distancing.

It was probably her own fault. The choices she'd made *definitely* were, and she'd never regretted those for a minute, but she did feel sometimes as if she'd missed the chance for connection. She'd never learned to talk about her work in the same way that other people talked about theirs. Partly she could blame the subject, but she'd had colleagues before who were able to talk about mycology to laypersons and not make their eyes glaze over, so maybe it was just her.

"I can't help it," she said, on the ground and in her own neighbourhood, with friends who were architects and bakers and school teachers – people with their own work stories, far less exciting than hers but able to bring in others and not exclude them by talking. "I was trained to talk about science this way!"

But then her architect friend had textbooks aplenty, too; the Antarctic Lichen had flipped through them once and seen a jargon to match that of her own discipline, but he could talk about his work, about the problems of art and material, in a way that the bakers and the school teachers could understand and join in on. The Antarctic Lichen could talk about shuttle launches and freeze-dried food, how it felt to look down on a planet from orbit, but the moment anyone asked her about lichen she fell back into science-talk.

An effective science communicator she was not. The Antarctic Lichen was the only astronaut who'd visited her friend's young class for talks and presentation, and still she was far and away the worst. As much as she loved her mycological experiments, it was a love that was frequently better silent – at least when not in the company of her peers.

It started early, at the university. Learning to write lab reports, learning to decipher papers. A mimicry of style, any small individualisms ironed out, to produce a prose of rigid objectivity shot through with words that, increasingly, only others in the same programme would ever understand. "The point of jargon is clarity," she heard, over and over, and it was clear enough for scientists, eventually, but absolute incomprehension for outsiders. "I think it's to make us look cleverer than we are," she'd argued, but the specificity of language continued, refining down to a point that only biologists were truly comfortable with, then botanists, and then mycologists.

By the time she'd finished her education, the Antarctic Lichen could reproduce that rigid style with the best of them and had half forgotten how to talk about her work – how to write about it – in any other way. And then it was field work, seasons of it, down on the ice and in other remote places, and all her companions were scientists doing the same thing, using the same language. They had a common tongue for their off-hours as well, but the breadth of conversation was never the same as when she'd gone home from lecture rooms to a flat full of people studying Russian literature or dance or education theory.

It wasn't that scientists were any less capable of talking about the arts than anyone else. It was just that she spent more time talking about the arts with them than she did with actual artists. It was enclosure that was the problem, because they all had the same voice to fall back on, the same voice they understood (and only they), and all of them were working on papers in that voice, reading to the others on the expedition and at the field sites, swapping analyses and shaving away anything that didn't conform to the standards of publication they'd been taught to reach for.

It was fascinating, in its way. Isolating, but fascinating, because of course the Antarctic Lichen could read her colleagues' work with the same attention and understanding as if it were Austen (though less funny) or Dickens (the same). Her excitement, inextricably, was linked with outside incomprehension, and the gulf between her life as a scientist and the lives outside that magic circle of science was a gaping thing (which she recognised, dimly) and a destructive one (which she didn't, not at first).

And then the Antarctic Lichen was an astronaut, on a space shuttle and then a space station, and she was even more cut off from the population that wasn't science, because there was the whole space of orbit between them and the only people she shared the space station with were scientists like herself. And then there were more scientists, and more, and they were setting off across a chasm to another world and the Antarctic Lichen watched them go and wondered how different it would be, the world created from a population base that was so much *of* science, absolutely isolated from the population of Earth both by distance and by vocation, homogeneous in a way that what they left behind was simply not.

The Antarctic Lichen watched them go, and wondered what that society would be. Wondered if she could find a place in it, a place where her own inability to communicate with people unlike her would be less hindrance than it was here . . . and wondered, too, if such an enclosure would even be good for her.

She'd been given the opportunity to apply. Had refused it, eventually, even in the confided knowledge that her application would be accepted. "I need something to struggle against," she'd said. Not understanding, really, why she'd said it, but aware of the fundamental truth of it.

They'd be too much like her, and similarity would not be enough for survival.

#

Although lichens can be intolerant of direct sunlight, some experimental work indicates that the Antarctic lichen is not stressed by insolation to the point of photoinhibition. However, in the absence of adequate water sources, observations in the field point to excessive summer sunlight potentially desiccating the lichen.

#

For all the inhibitive effects of isolation, the Antarctic Lichen hadn't considered the potential risk that the lure of freedom from it might pose. She'd known of the Stone Wētā long before the woman came aboard – she'd had to know, to have the data sets ready to pass on to her. But it was a tactless admission, that wētā tattoo. Provocation all through. A new addition, as far as the Antarctic Lichen could judge, and one that would have been beyond foolish to share on the planet below. Here…

The Antarctic Lichen didn't grudge any colonist their reminders – it was a one-way trip for all of them, and the ecosystem they were leaving behind would never be experienced again.

"Of course it's all going anyway," she'd heard one of them say, the gruff words at odds with the wistful stare down at oceans. The rising oceans, the increasing deserts. The shape of continents might remain, those that weren't altered too badly by rising sea levels, but the small environments they'd loved in, were raised in, and the creatures they'd shared those environments with . . .

Some organisms had gone with the colonists – seeds, microorganisms, small invertebrates. But there were no fish, no birds. None of the larger animals that still clung to existence in the wilder corners of the world. No whales, no elephants. Not even domestic animals – dogs or sheep or cats. They took nothing that wouldn't be useful, nothing that couldn't be provided for.

So it was no surprise that reminders were taken for place and creature. The tattoo might have been that, if the Antarctic Lichen didn't already know what it represented: the ability to survive in harsh environments, to hibernate out of sight, buried in rock, until the advent of a warmer time. To bring that into sunlight, to ink it into skin as an advertisement, ran the risk of a harsher scrutiny than might be healthy. Isolation was one thing. Daylight another, and the Antarctic Lichen both admired the act and feared the consequences of it.

No matter how careful the Stone Wētā had been, if there was any suspicion of her role prior to that tattoo there would have been plenty after. Discretion probably meant that the Stone Wētā had avoided other operatives in her last days on Earth, but the Antarctic Lichen was not on Earth, and she had her own scrutiny to avoid, her own continued isolation to navigate, and she was not prepared for the sustained glare of artificial light.

#

The Antarctic lichen grows extraordinarily slowly; it averages only a fraction of a millimetre each year. Decades-long monitoring of the lichen at various polar sites shows a measurable difference in growth rates between these sites, and the relative age of each population is subsequently established, assuming a constant rate of growth at each site. This indicates that some populations are older than others, which in turn suggests that the younger populations are the result of later colonisation, after climate changes affected snowfall patterns and made new substrates available for potential colonisation by the lichen. Thus the presence and history of the Antarctic lichen is itself a means of establishing a climate record.

#

It was hard to be an astronaut and not be an environmentalist. Even the engineers, the physicists, those payload specialists who had nothing to do with the study and subject of life, found themselves at windows staring down, their expressions painted over with Earth-shine and wonder. The Antarctic Lichen had done so herself. Still did it, and each time she looked she felt as the others did a sense of the absolute fragility of biosphere, the ease with which it could be taken away.

"It's strange," she said to one of her fellow astronauts. "The station itself is a far frailer construct. Far more vulnerable, far easier to destroy. Yet when I look down it's as if I've forgotten what I'm standing on, and all that acknowledgement of vulnerability just fades away. Transfers from the station to the planet."

"That's because we can always build another station," he said. "We can't build another planet." The loss of the former would be a setback for the space industry, a small tragedy in the history of exploration, but the loss of the latter would be catastrophic. Even the distant colonisation of a second planet could never make up for the lack of the first, the destruction of a biosphere that was as far as anyone knew unparalleled in the universe.

She'd understood that rarity for the first time, aboard the station – really understood it, with heart instead of head. "It's like that for everyone," she was told, as the station commander welcomed her aboard, smiling at the overwhelmed expression on her face.

The Antarctic Lichen had always been an environmentalist. She'd seen the photos – Earthrise and The Blue Marble – known the watershed impact they'd had on the conservation movement. Had expected to feel that impact again, and magnified, in her first glimpse of the planet from orbit, but expectation and emotional preparation had failed to give her the first hint of the enormity of her response.

"It's so much more than I imagined," she'd said. Her life was split into two at that moment: everything before she'd looked down at Earth from orbit, and everything after. She tried to explain it to her friends, to journalists, to school children, and failed. The disturbance event of her life, and the old life swept away.

The photos had done that for a different generation, but that early promise had been squandered, their effects less than total. The Antarctic Lichen had had her eyes opened in orbit, but that was an option open to very few, and all of them, after, were sympathetic.

She'd never hidden the drives after that. Not that there was anywhere she could have hidden them from determined searching. The station was too enclosed, too remote. There was only the one cache – to be sent with the colonists, and after that her involvement was over. The Antarctic Lichen had planned to offer again, when back on Earth. To find a place that no-one else could, in the rocks and Dry Valleys where she knew her possibilities best. But the Stone Wētā might have taken that chance away, because if her identity was known now then there were very few options for those who could have passed a package onwards.

It was plausible, perhaps, that there were more than one of the data operatives on their way to Mars, and that she'd be cleared from suspicion thereby. Plausible, too, that they'd each taken with them their own small packets of information. That a movement had gone towards Mars as much as an individual . . . the Antarctic Lichen hoped it had. Hoped that the Stone Wētā's gesture had a purpose behind it more than baiting, a final flip-off.

If not, the Antarctic Lichen might have been side-lined for nothing.

She'd accept that side-lining if she had to. Had been a co-author more than two dozen times, and knew from the experience that each person had their part to play, and that trying to hog the process was often counter-productive.

"I'm grateful for what I've been able to do," she said, staring down at blue water and trying to convince herself that gratitude was all she felt.

#

Although the Antarctic lichen is highly adapted to cold and aridity, it can be killed by too much of either. The lichen requires regular summer snow melt, and the absence of or severe reduction in snowfall will not provide sufficient water. Alternately, although the lichen can survive being buried beneath even relatively deep snow in winter, increased or particularly lengthy periods of snow cover can lead to a phenomenon known as "snowkill", which is a factor in lichen death. Geographic regions that are susceptible to either of these extremes frequently have younger populations, as periodic snowkills and water loss inhibit the continued existence of earlier lichens.

#

The Antarctic Lichen was used to dangerous environments. It was part of the reason she spent so much of her working life enclosed with other scientists – on the ice, on the launch pad. She'd had her share of accidents, some of them minor, some of them not. Twice her life had been at risk: once when her vehicle had failed in the polar valleys and left her and her team stranded in a sudden storm. They'd survived only because their equipment was good enough to keep hypothermia at bay before rescue, but it had been a near thing.

The second was when her suit failed.

Not a death anyone would have wanted, floating in vacuum. She'd survived only because her partner on the spacewalk risked his own life, pushing his own equipment past tolerance to drag her back. She was shaking for hours afterwards, wrapped in blankets and being fed warm drinks while arguments raged about her.

"They're calling it a sudden catastrophic failure," said the station commander, of the response from the ground. "An accident." All of the astronauts assigned to the station were gathered together, crammed in one room – representatives of six different nationalities and twice as many disciplines. "I don't believe it for one fucking second."

"You're not the only one. Doesn't mean it couldn't have been one of us who did it. Sabotaged her suit."

"This was my first time wearing it up here," said the Antarctic Lichen, reiterating what they all knew. She didn't have to say anything else. If she'd had a successful spacewalk with it before, it would give weight to the sabotage argument, but the six of them were logicians all through and, although accident was still a possibility, probability allowed for more than one option; and the only other option was interference on the ground.

"I don't believe it was any of us, either," said the commander. "It still could be an accident. I don't much credit it, but it could be. And I think you know why I don't."

"I don't know what you mean," said the Antarctic Lichen.

"Oh, please. You're hardly subtle. And it's not like there's a lot of room to hide here."

"We all know," said the man who'd saved her life. "Why d'you think I was keeping such a close eye on you out there? The five of us hear the rumours too." And were more inclined than most to believe them, to *want* to believe, because they looked down from heights as well, understood fragility and sacrifice, the ease with which one could be destroyed and the other offered up.

"We talked about it, all of us. We're not asking for details. It's best if you don't trust us with them, probably." In case one of them was a traitor to science, to the planet that turned below –

and betrayal existed. If someone on the ground had engineered that suit to fail, it was a scientist with more than one master – and there'd been enough of them, over the years, in different fields and with different compromises. Climate was only the latest confrontation, and some people fell to power no matter their training in method and scepticism.

"You've saved my life," said the Antarctic Lichen, just as she'd said it as a young woman to the rescue party on the ice, who'd come for her field team because they were scientists, too, and might one day need their own rescuing from bright places. "I think that's trust enough."

That first rescue had happened long before she'd ever heard of wētā, back when snowkill was still a new and inexperienced part of her vocabulary. It was uncompromised intent, and it struck her then that for some that generosity could still survive.

"You can't risk it," said the commander. "We're agreed on that." He glanced out the window, to the only thing seen from that window any of them ever looked at. "The consequence of any betrayal would be too high," he said. "We're not prepared to pay it."

#

Because of its particular snow-related requirements, the Antarctic lichen is often found growing either on horizontal surfaces, or surfaces that are only mildly inclined and moderately unshaded. This is because the lichen's thallus needs sufficient opportunity to hydrate. If the substrate is too consistently shaded, the sun is not able to melt the snow on top of it, and if the substrate is too inclined the melting snow is liable to slip off it before fully hydrating the lichen.

#

The Antarctic Lichen hadn't realised how much she'd come to stifle under the weight of secrecy until she didn't have to anymore. "I understand your reservations," she said, and honoured them by not talking about her contacts, by not making any reference to specificity or anything that could be considered a possible trail. But they were scientists, her station mates, and they knew the language of science in ways that laypeople did not, and that training made them comfortable with the hypothetical, and with the history of ethical behaviour expected from (and sometimes failed by) other scientists.

"Of course we can talk about how we might protect data as well," said one of them. "It's only a *theory*." A phrase they'd all heard far too often, in different contexts, and universally hated.

"I can't tell you how often I've tried to explain what a bloody theory is," said the Antarctic Lichen, laughing, but it was a bitter laughter. "I'm not sure it's ever sunk in."

"Some people just don't want to understand."

That was the problem, distilled. The apotheosis of ignorance, the desire not to know and to valorise the not knowing. The willingness, too, to be bought, and scientists were susceptible to this as well as others. There was immunisation of sorts in the training, the privilege of objectivity and the acknowledged problem of bias.

"It's not just that," said the Antarctic Lichen. "We're to blame as well. For not explaining better, for not doing better." All those things that scientists had done in the past – the monstrosities they'd built, the things they'd exploited for learning and some of those things the living. She was all too aware of her own failures. "If we'd done better then we wouldn't have to hide now." If they'd been better teachers, better activists. If they'd protested the shutting down of science classes more, if they hadn't turned to other problems when kids were being trained not to be sceptical, not to test for truth and weakness. If they'd worked harder to keep politicians who didn't understand science and didn't want to out of power, politicians beholden to special interests who'd make laws to protect those interests, who'd gut environmental regulations and research funding, stifle information, do their best to promote a compliant citizenry.

"It's our fault," she said. "We failed."

"It's not only our fault. Other people failed too, and worse."

"This isn't the world I grew up dreaming of," said the Antarctic Lichen. She'd dreamed of polar laboratories and planetary colonisation, scientists of all stripes coming together for exploration. She'd lived those dreams too, been part of them even if her involvement in the colonisation was peripheral, a waystation of sorts. "Thing is, it was *all* I imagined. The science, isolated. I didn't think of the world around it, any sort of social context. I dreamed of labs and shuttles and expeditions, the places I'd go out into. I didn't think of how to bring other people with me."

Now it was all she could think about, and the danger such sharing might put her in. She wasn't bound to the station forever – would have to go back down to Earth soon, into a world where knowledge of her role wouldn't be a protection, as it had come to be up here, where those who knew had been made to sympathise by sight of home. It was the old saw all over again – daylight as disinfectant. But the Antarctic Lichen had enough experience of light now that she knew it could burn (and burn profoundly) as well as purify.

"It can also set things alight," said the station commander, standing with her, looking down. "Lately when I stand here I feel more a soldier than a scientist," he said. (The spreading desert, the rising tide. The absence of ice.)

"We've got to learn better ways to fight," said the Antarctic Lichen.

"Fighting is what I'm afraid of," he replied.

The Antarctic Lichen took his hand, looked away from planet and into void, remembering the shock of her potential murder. It would have come from spite, mostly, for all her work had then been done – or so she'd thought. "Me too," she said.

THE GLASS SPONGE

The glass sponge is not a species. It is a class of animals found in all oceans, although they are particularly prevalent in Antarctica. A high proportion of the glass sponges found in Antarctic waters are endemic to that environment. The Polar Front of the Antarctic Circumpolar Current helps to isolate the southern biota, and the ecology that builds up in that isolation is one that is unused to incursion and non-polar threats.

#

The Glass Sponge hated when visitors came to Scott Base. She supposed it was ungenerous of her – distrustful, and unwelcoming – but for all her desire to share the science of her days with people who were unfamiliar with it, she could never keep from suspecting their motives.

It was an open secret, more or less, among those who worked down in Antarctica that a southern cache of climate data was stashed nearby the Base, smuggled out of countries whose administrations preferred to purge their science than rely upon it. An open secret, as well, that one of the operatives responsible for that cache worked at the Base, though who she was – and her code name – was unconfirmed, if suspected. And while the Glass Sponge didn't know all of the dozens of permanent staff there, at least not well enough for confidence, she was confident in enough of them to know that they would have come to her if they guessed anything threatening of their co-workers.

It had happened once before. A meteorologist had pulled her aside late one afternoon, when she was checking dive equipment in preparation for the next day's work. "The new guy," the other scientist had said. "The one with the ice core team? I don't know anything for certain, but there's something about him. About the questions he's been asking. I don't know what he's after and I don't care to know . . . just watch yourself, alright?"

The Glass Sponge had done exactly that, been as vague and as scatty as she could get away with, done everything she could to make herself look too silly to be a threat. The scientists she trusted rolled their eyes and went along, made a game of it – she overheard their made-up complaints, observed with quiet malice the all-too-obvious rolling of the eyes when she entered a room the ice core interloper was already in – and when the season was over that interloper went home, she hoped, with nothing.

"Good bloody riddance," she said, under her breath, but that minor discretion was undermined when congratulatory beers came her way at dinner and she couldn't stop herself from smirking.

"You look like you swallowed the canary," said one of the astronomers, smirking himself.

"A cold and lonely little canary," said the Glass Sponge. "Too frozen to swallow. Hopped his way off the ice, heading for home."

But they kept coming, the quiet and the questioning. It was never the ones she could see who bothered her; mostly people weren't anywhere near as subtle as they thought (and that was a terrifying thought for a woman who prided herself on a certain subtle capacity of her own) and the Glass Sponge could spot them well enough. If she wasn't certain she treated them as if she were, because that way lay safety and if they were any sort of honest scientist they wouldn't begrudge her scepticism. It was the ones she couldn't pick that bothered her – and she knew they were there, worming their way in. Noting who disappeared when and where, narrowing down who was doing the caching.

It could even be one of the people she trusted. The Glass Sponge wasn't foolish enough to think herself infallible but she had a duty to science above that which saw her examining the polar biota, and she couldn't let herself be frightened into immobility, couldn't keep second-guessing loyalties. That and paranoia would drive her mad, so she smiled when the people she trusted took sudden, diversionary trips of their own onto the ice, buggering off for the afternoon with no clear purpose.

"I was just off for a walk," said Dave, said Lexi and Marama and Bill. "You never know what you can find out there!"

Dave's shit-eating grin was particularly effective.

"You bloody stirrer," said the Glass Sponge, after he'd made a target of himself one day in the dining hall. There was snickering over the dinner plates, someone snorting into their cup. "You are all bloody stirrers."

"I hope they go home thinking *everyone* here's in on it," said

Marama. "I hope they're so damn confused they never come back." But that was wishful thinking.

Wishful thinking, too, were the dark jokes about not going home at all. "I told him to look out for the leopard seals," said Bill. "You've seen him, contrary bugger. Didn't pay any attention, thought I was just yanking his chain. Realised just a bit too early he was being stalked."

"Shame," said the Glass Sponge, but beneath the bravado she wasn't sure if she would have celebrated a death. It might have made things easier in the short run, might have smacked of justice, even, that an operative so intent on supporting those who were doing their damnedest to encourage ecological collapse came to a carnivorous end. But there'd have been questions, more of them and less silent than before – and the suspicion that the death hadn't been accidental, that there was someone down on the Base who dealt in murder as well as espionage.

It disturbed her that her most compelling argument against murder was a practical one. The Glass Sponge wanted to think herself more moral than that, but the disappearances so far were so one-sided – climate scientists she knew only by code names, and from whispers – that her own mental landscape took on ever more of the patina of war.

"Still, it's only six more weeks he's here," she said. "Best he goes back unharmed. I don't want to sound paranoid, but if people start disappearing on the ice there's no guarantee it'll stop at them."

She'd risk her own life for data, but she wasn't going to be risking anyone else's.

"Isn't that our decision to make?" said Lexi. A conservator

assigned to assist in the restoration of historic huts, she understood the need for preservation as well as anybody – and it was a valid question, but not one that the Glass Sponge could answer without confirming that she was the Sand Cat's southernmost operative. They suspected, on the Base, but they didn't *know* – even her friends, the people she most trusted, couldn't say with absolute certainty that she was the reason the search was drawing closer.

There was no good way to answer, and so she didn't . . . but the Glass Sponge knew that silence could also be taken as confirmation, in its way.

#

The glass sponges are community organisms. Their spicules are siliceous, tiny sharp pieces of skeleton that weave together to form spicule mats. These may be as many as several metres deep, and provide structural support for the sponge. The mats are also a protective habitat for many small invertebrates, a locking-together of spongy skeleton that helps to keep marine predators away.

#

She woke the next morning to a confirmation come from silence regardless, a confirmation come with intrusion and shaking and with sound instead of light. A hand on her arm, a whisper in her ear. "Mate," she heard, "mate, you've got to wake up."

The door was closed very quietly, and there was a small

scuffling noise that the Glass Sponge recognised as someone fumbling for a switch. When the light came on she blinked hard, and if the weight in her stomach wasn't sharp enough for panic yet, it was close, because the Glass Sponge had been waiting for the other shoe to drop for some time now, had fallen asleep every night under the shadow of nets and quiet drawings-in.

Lexi was at the door, her back pressed against it, and her eyes were wide in her face. Dave was crouched down beside the bed, his hands grasping her shoulders. "What?" said the Glass Sponge. "What's happened?"

"Sinclair's dead," said Dave, his mouth set in grim lines, and the Glass Sponge felt cold horror wash over her. Frank Sinclair, the latest visitor, and she was certain in her bones that he'd come looking for climate data – for the person who was hiding it.

"Please tell me it was an accident," she said, but the clock beside her bed showed it was only a quarter to four, and no accident was likely to befall anyone lying in their bed at that hour.

"Stabbed," said Dave. "Stabbed outside, too – what he was doing out there I don't know, but he dragged himself back into the vehicle bay and that's where he died. There's blood everywhere. No chance it was natural."

"Shit," said the Glass Sponge. "Shit, shit, *shit!*" It was unmitigated disaster. "Who found him?"

"Evan," said Lexi, naming the astronomer who had teased the Glass Sponge about canaries and victory, and who had a habit of wandering the station in the early hours. "He saw a door open and went to investigate."

"Shit," said the Glass Sponge again, and reached for a shirt.

Dave snatched it off her. "Don't get up," he said. "Go back to sleep – pretend you have, at any rate," he amended, seeing her disbelieving expression. "Evan woke Lexi, and he's giving it ten minutes before he goes to wake the head."

"He shouldn't have done that," said the Glass Sponge. It was a risk to wait; it could only cause suspicion to fall on him if anyone ever found out about the delay.

"He's doing what he has to," said Dave, and there was no discussion then of loyalties and consequences, because they could all see the storm that was coming down upon them, the dark and looming shape of it. "Lexi came to get me—"

"He was awake anyway, I could hear him moving around—"

"And we came to warn you. Don't look like that, Evan knew we would. Look, your poker face is good but it's not that good."

"I don't know what you're talking about," said the Glass Sponge, automatic in her denials, but it impressed neither of them.

"Whatever. There'll be an announcement in a couple of hours, probably. We didn't reckon it was a good idea for anyone to catch you off guard."

"*If* you were off guard," said Lexi, and the Glass Sponge stared hard at her with narrow eyes.

"I've been in my bed all night," she said.

"You just keep telling people that," said Lexi. "We all need to be in our beds right now, and all night is where we've been there. Just remember to look shocked in the morning."

"That won't be hard," said the Glass Sponge. "I *am* shocked. We're all going to be shocked."

"Not all of us," said Dave, and it was only after he left that the implication of his words struck the Glass Sponge, quivering in her nest of blankets with the room closing in around her.

Five of them, when the head began to speak, would not be shocked. Herself, Dave, Lexi. Evan. And whoever it was that killed Sinclair.

She cried a little beneath the blankets, silently, and hoped like hell that it was indeed five people who knew. Five, and not four.

The Glass Sponge was under no illusions that her hands would be seen as clean. She also thought that a significant number of the people who suspected her would frankly not care if she had done it. Murder was a terrible thing, but self-defence was an excuse anyone would cling to and the disappearances, the so-called accidental deaths of climate scientists, were a whispered and half-known thing. She'd had enough veiled warnings, had enough of her colleagues come up to her and pretend casual conversation – some better and some worse at the pretending – in which they made it clear that while they knew nothing, they'd hate to see anything happen to someone who did. The tacit support, while sometimes irritating, had been a comfort. The scientists who turned up unexpectedly to chat while she was alone with Sinclair, or with a Sinclair equivalent, had made it clear that she was being watched out for, that her exposure to danger was being deliberately ameliorated by community, and by community values . . . but this was an amelioration too far.

The Glass Sponge *had* been asleep. She had killed no-one. Which meant either that someone had killed on her behalf, or that there was another person here, another one who worked for the Sand Cat, and that person had seen a threat to themselves and removed it.

She almost hoped for that. The Glass Sponge would have been glad to know that she had missed a friend, a shadow-colleague, that she had been so thoroughly hoodwinked. Because if she hadn't, if she was indeed the only woman at Scott Base smuggling climate data, then she had a friend who had compromised themselves for her, compromised themselves hideously and in more ways than one.

The Glass Sponge did not know how to live with the enormity of such a gift.

#

In some Antarctic waters the increase in glass sponge population is attributed to more than sunlight. Starfish are typical predators of the sponges but this predation is reduced by ocean acidification. The starfish, finding themselves in waters grown too sharp for them, cannot compete. The acid water makes them eat less, makes them grow and spread more slowly. They find it difficult to adapt to the hostile environment around them, and even periods of acclimation are no remedy.

#

"You're not asking if I did it," said Lexi.

"I'm not asking if anyone did it," said the Glass Sponge. "Truthfully, I'm not sure that I want to know." That was a lie. She did want to know – and so would the Sand Cat, because whoever had done this had exposed them all to a level of scrutiny that would be difficult to manage.

The Glass Sponge supposed that she should have expected it. The climate cache in Antarctica was well suspected. That it was administered by someone out of Scott Base was just as well known. Hell, at least half the Base thought that it was her. They didn't have any *proof* of her involvement – she'd never given them any – but stupid people, on the whole, weren't recruited to the ice. She lived in a small, enclosed community of individuals who had developed the skills to sift evidence, to construct hypotheses and test for fit, and they didn't suddenly lose those skills when faced with personalities instead of polar geology or hydrodynamics.

So, no proof, but the Glass Sponge believed from her own observations that she was far and away the most likely source. She pretended ignorance on a regular basis, taking on the perception of an uninvolved party, sifting through her colleagues and herself to see who came off most convincingly as someone to be suspected. She imagined herself a newcomer to the Base, and tried to picture that newcomer's first days, their first interactions, and how they would take the moving pieces of that small community and build them into a picture of responsibility and guilt.

Every time, that construct of innocent personality would finger herself as the person most likely to hide data. The Glass Sponge believed that this conclusion was influenced by the certain knowledge of her own role, but she also knew that this might not account for all of her imaginings. Truth was, she'd been careless. Oh, she'd never admitted anything outright – but she'd never had to. The speculation had been amusing to her, and she'd shown her amusement, knowing all the while that for some it would be evidence enough of complicity.

"Don't you wonder who it is?" said Lexi.

"We're all wondering that," said the Glass Sponge. There were hushed conversations in every corner, conversations that came to a sudden halt when she entered the room. People she had hoped would have known her better were eyeing her speculatively.

"It's not just you they're staring at," said Marama over breakfast.

"Sure feels like it," said the Glass Sponge, and Marama had put down her spoon, given her a long quiet look.

"Don't let paranoia make you look guilty," she said, and while the Glass Sponge could credit the wisdom of that advice she couldn't help but think that Marama had meant *look more guilty*.

She was absolutely aware that she looked guilty as hell.

#

A glass sponge can freeze under observation. Some exhibit no measurable growth for over 20 years. This changes with the introduction of a new environmental factor – for instance, when the removal of shading sea ice (the calving of a massive iceberg, the melting of shelves) prompts an increase in phytoplankton. This rise in available food sources is a catalyst for the glass sponge, and its growth moves again from stasis.

#

The one bright spot about one of the first ever murders on Antarctic soil was that there was no lack of publicity. The Base was isolated, somewhat, from the worst of it – there were no journalists turning up at the door, no cameras flashing in anyone's face – but the news was well and truly out there. This meant that the Glass Sponge didn't need to contact the Sand Cat to warn her of the coming storm. The Sand Cat, wherever she was, had access to world news and even if she didn't know the level of her operative's involvement, or the true role of the victim, she knew that attention would be drawn. Contact between the two women was severed.

The Glass Sponge had an alternate channel, one set up for her to use in the event her first was compromised, but she was reluctant to use it. One way or another, she'd be under investigation and there'd be no more data coming her way, not for the foreseeable future and perhaps not ever again.

There was a certain black humour in her isolation, and it was a humour informed by vocation. The glass sponges of Antarctica were notoriously slow-growing, but with the warming world and the collapse of shading ice shelves they were receiving more sunlight than before and their growth rate had become enormous, a comparative explosion of development.

Unlike her subjects, however, the Glass Sponge had to freeze under sunlight. Daylight was supposed to be a disinfectant for dodgy behaviour and for her, increased scrutiny meant sterilisation and the deliberate removal of anything beneath the surface. All her concerns now had to appear superficial – her biological research, the concern for a murdered colleague.

Even if the people around her didn't buy it, the people coming to investigate would need to.

"What's going to happen to me?" she said.

"Don't think like that." Dave shook his head. "There's no

proof you did it."

The Glass Sponge was grateful that he just assumed there was no proof – no fibres, no blood spatter. No murder weapon with her fingerprints on it. No murder weapon at all, for the knife – if it was a knife, or just something sharp and capable of stabbing – had yet to be found.

"What else could there be?" he continued. "Yeah, there are people here who think you've been hiding data but that's all it is. Thoughts. And you're not the only one people suspect." They'd put targets on themselves, him and the other three. Her particular friends, going off alone for walks, trying to spread suspicion around. "It could be any of us," he said. "Don't admit anything. Play dumb."

"It's not going to be hard to play dumb when I don't know anything," the Glass Sponge remarked. She hoped it sounded convincing, because the things she knew and didn't know intersected in difficult and unrewarding ways.

It was the same for others, and she increasingly felt herself as the point of intersection. Relations with McMurdo Station, usually so cordial, came to take on patterns of freeze-thaw. It too was a place of scientists and there should have been sympathy, but Sinclair had been one of theirs in nationality if not in spirit and the Glass Sponge held no illusions that the senior administrators at the other Station hadn't been placed by those with fundamentally different priorities. There'd be few who had sympathy for caching there, and fewer still who wouldn't want Sinclair's killer caught.

McMurdo was only three kilometres from Scott Base, the station of a superpower rather than a small South Pacific nation and she'd never felt the distance so closely before. Not even when she was out at the cache, securing new data in a lockbox hidden in the ice, had the Glass Sponge felt so watched.

"It's not in my head, is it?" she said to Bill as the investigation continued, hoping for accusations of paranoia. The most laid-back of her friends, the one she always counted on not to panic.

"No," he said. "Not anymore." He started to reach out and thought better of it, but his eyes were sympathetic. "Can you get out?" he said.

The Glass Sponge shook her head. "I don't know what you're talking about," she said. Plausible deniability might have been shot on her own account, but she'd be damned if she'd let the suspicion of new collusion, of shared knowledge, fall on anyone else.

It fell anyway, when Lexi admitted to the murder. "Why'd you do it?" she was asked, and she'd looked them straight back in the eye, those investigators who were as compromised as she was.

"You know why," she said. It was all she'd say before she was taken away.

Dave came to the Glass Sponge later that night, walking as if there was sickness in him. "It wasn't her," he said. "She said she heard me awake, but we were together that night. You know." He was married, had a wife back home in Whangarei. "It was only the once. But it wasn't her. It couldn't have been."

The Glass Sponge wept bitterly in her bed. There was no use asking why. "You know why," Lexi had said – had known, too, that without a more obvious culprit it would have been the Glass Sponge who was taken away, and one more front in the climate war would have quietly crumbled.

47

Against the planet, one person was a small price.

Against herself it was an enormous one.

"I never said it was me," she said, in the break room, in the station. People left her alone after that, because either she'd taken the credit for something that wasn't hers or she'd let a friend take credit instead.

She still didn't know who'd done it.

It was six months before the Glass Sponge returned to the cache. The Sand Cat had re-opened communications – a cautious reaching out that spoke of desperation and limited options, for no-one had heard from Lexi since she'd been taken away and hers wasn't the only disappearance. There was new data to hide, a copy of a copy in case all the others were hunted down, and the Glass Sponge clutched the small drive to her chest and skittered along the ice, careful in her absence. Trying not to draw suspicion.

She retrieved the lockbox, opened it up for stashing, and the world that was already so frozen around her froze a little more, for it was science in the box beneath her fingers, and truth, the hope for a future world, and its preservation had made her a liar.

"Some scientist you are," she said, and set the data in the box, covered it over again with ice enough to block out the sunlight.

THE RESURRECTION PLANT

Photosynthetic recovery in the resurrection plant is linked not only to the reintroduction of water but to temperature. Recovery is inhibited at both low and high degrees, with an optimal recovery temperature of 25° Celsius. Although the resurrection plant can survive increasing droughts, longer and hotter periods are a threat to the ability that gives the plant its name.

#

Root systems went deep in the desert.

They had to. The desert was drying out, with the river system over-allocated for agriculture and the aquifers emptying. Plants that were already adapted to aridity were getting more of it, testing their tolerance levels, and too-heavy grazing by farm animals was putting ever more strain on the softer, non-woody species.

Resurrection moved slowly through a small corner of desert, inspecting, cataloguing. Supervising as well, because she had two interns surveying with her. The Chihuahuan Desert had potentially the greatest biodiversity of the Earth deserts – of any desert, she would have said once, but the recent colonisation of Mars was a reminder that other worlds held other deserts, and that she was not the only one to wonder. But that diversity was more and more at risk as the climate changed, and Resurrection was back in the desert, monitoring species abundance and ecological transformation. She couldn't survey the whole desert, of course, but her work at the Maderas del Carmen protected area was supported by a small number of field workers, university students who she rotated through a number of field sites, hoping to build a picture of change over time. Some of those students were trained enough to work on their own now, but the newest pair were still learning ecological technique.

"Look at the birds circling," said Teresa, standing and staring at the sky with her hands at the base of her back, stiff from squatting.

"If it's not got roots I don't care," Verónica replied. She was poring over a field guide, looking from page to plant and back again. Resurrection was watching her from the corner of her eye, waiting to see if she needed help in her classifications.

"It's not far. I'm going to see if I can find it," the other girl replied, and Resurrection let her go. She'd been working well, and she'd selected interns for their curiosity after all. Ten minutes later, when she heard the screams for help and saw Teresa crouched over a fallen figure, she was grateful for her choice.

The woman was covered in dirt, and what colour showed

beneath the dust was red. Sunburn and blood, for her feet were bare and torn to shreds, her hands and knees scraped raw where she had fallen.

"She's alive," said Verónica, her fingers searching a limp wrist for a pulse. "But she's not sweating."

Resurrection had experienced heat exhaustion herself, once, back when she was younger even than her students. She'd grown up in the desert, assumed her knowledge of it would save her and she'd been careless, over-confident. It was a mistake she'd only made the once, but she'd made sure, afterwards, to relearn the first aid for exhaustion and worse, and she'd never forgotten it, the knowledge lying deep within her and only needing opportunity to reassert itself.

They were lucky to be surveying in a place that, if remote, still had accessible water. Ecological restoration efforts in the area included the installation of a number of wildlife-friendly water troughs. Not perfect but, hours away from the nearest settlement, those troughs were the best option.

Resurrection dumped the contents of her water bottle over the unconscious woman, soaking the remains of her clothes as much as she could, before lifting her legs. "Loosen her clothes. Everything you can. Take an arm each, we need to get her to the truck." The three of them together could manage easily, and once the woman was laid out in the back seat with Teresa jammed in with her, fanning her frantically with a clipboard, Resurrection drove as fast as she could to the trough they'd passed on their way in.

It was only a couple of kilometres back, and once the woman was in the water Resurrection worked to prop up her head so her face was out of the water, her fingers and feet floating to the surface. "We need shade," she said. "Rig up what you can from what's in the vehicle. *Don't* use your own clothes," she added, as Teresa began to pull off the loose shirt she wore over her tank. "I don't want two of you to look after."

Even with a tarpaulin tented over to keep out the worst of the sun, the water still wasn't truly cold. "Keep fanning," said Resurrection. "It'll evaporate the water on her face and extremities, make her cool faster."

She had one of the girls radio for help. It was the best she could do. Resurrection didn't see much chance for survival, but there would certainly have been none if she'd waited to cool the woman and driven her out of the desert instead. Instead she sat with her legs under the woman's head, sprinkling water over her face and fanning her, talking to her in a low calm voice and noting, as her clothes rippled in the water, the injuries beneath.

"It's working!"said Verónica, her cheeks pink with exertion under her hat, as the woman shifted and moaned against them, her eyes opening. "She's getting better!"

"She's barely conscious," said Resurrection. She didn't want to discourage Verónica, but the woman's clouded gaze did not speak much of recovery to her. "She doesn't know where she is."

Her own experience with dehydration and heat had been a much kinder thing. A reminder of foolishness, yes, but she was bred to the environment here in a way that the injured woman simply wasn't. Her flesh was too pale, blistered raw with sunburn, layers of epidermis peeling in sheets. It hurt to look at her. And when the woman's eyes opened again, wandering, almost insensible, her fragments of speech showed by her accent just how foreign she was.

"The bristlecone pine lives for thousands of years," she whispered, and Resurrection started and felt the shock, again, of her own water-filled recovery, back when the world had been a cooler place.

#

The resurrection plant curls in on itself during periods of dryness. The reduced surface area of the curled plant helps to limit light-induced damage during desiccation, making it easier for the plant to recover photosynthetic ability when moisture returns. The protection against photoinhibition isn't total, as light damage still occurs before the curling is complete, and if the resurrection plant is somehow prevented from curling, the photosynthetic recovery of the plant is significantly and negatively affected.

#

Science had taught her not to trust in coincidence. Oh, it happened often enough, Resurrection knew. Sometimes it even happened to her: the email from a friend she was just about to write to, the song she was humming suddenly playing on the radio. She wasn't the sort to assign a deeper meaning to random occurrences, aware as she was of the many coincidences that didn't occur, the events that didn't draw her attention or bias. A random encounter didn't have to mean anything. It could have been coincidence that a woman who spoke of bristlecone pines was found by one who spoke of resurrection plants. She could be making connections where none existed, and there was no certainty, even, that the woman she'd found in the desert had knowledge in her of more than tree rings.

But. There was too much to discount, and too much risk in the discounting. An injured woman, dumped in the desert – there was no way she'd walked there, not in her condition – and with injuries that a cursory glance could see were layered under the effects of exposure and sunlight. When Resurrection looked at her, when she even *thought* of her, she heard the sound of rain. Of drops in the desert, waiting to be taken up so that movement could be observed, the unfurling of a close and secret thing.

Resurrection had never felt less like movement in her life. Had never felt more the power and potential of observation, and what it was like to be the subject of it.

You're making it more than it needs to be, she thought to herself, washing her hands in the bathroom that night, after the woman had been taken away to hospital, and herself questioned and left. But she was aware as she thought that it *was* a thought, and not something to be spoken aloud. She stared at her face in the mirror as she washed, trying to find a balance in expression that wavered between worry and a too-careful blankness. Some anxiety would be expected, a normal concern for a stranger she'd tried to help, but Resurrection, watching her own reaction, was afraid in the curled-up, camouflaged centre of herself that she wasn't the only one watching for it.

Paranoia. It had to be – something to be accepted and navigated regardless of Bristlecone Pine, wherever she might be. Something that could help her, if she were careful.

Without paranoia, she might have been tempted to contact the Sand Cat. A simple message, a single phrase, and the Sand Cat would have warning. But all warnings were raindrops, and if that woman alone in the desert had been meant to prompt her into action then there might be others who were looking to see where the water left a stain.

Without paranoia, she might have made herself believe in coincidence, and mistaken identity. Might have made herself forget the burn marks she saw beneath sunburn, the damage of one bright heat hidden by another.

I'll risk myself if I have to, she thought, tucked into her own bed and with her eyes closed, breathing slowly and deeply as if asleep, because survival now was the stillness of desert waiting.

She could not risk the Sand Cat.

There was more, too, that she could not risk. Data that she could not now retrieve, wondering as she was if someone was watching. Data that she had to hide, wondering all the while if someone was coming for it.

Wondering, too, how much was known and how much was only guessed. Resurrection wasn't the only scientist working in the Chihuahuan Desert, and she'd had no interaction with Bristlecone herself, known of her only from what another operative had said in passing. It didn't mean the other woman didn't know her, but the possibility, she thought, was lessened.

They'd worked in the desert for weeks, Teresa and Verónica and herself. The field work had been planned in advance, their dates and destinations logged. It wasn't a secret. It was possible, she thought, that someone could have dropped the woman into an area close to their study site, relying on the actions of animals to draw attention to her. Simple enough if it was meant as a threat – but a simplicity that relied on death, on the impossibility of communication.

If the woman in the desert was Bristlecone Pine, if she lived to talk about how she got there, then the capacity for threat was diminished. There'd be investigation, prosecution, perhaps, of the people who dumped her. Living, she was a loose end. Whether she was left that way deliberately, in hopes that she'd wash out further operatives, was the question. It was the only thing Resurrection could think of that made any sense – why dump her alive at all, unless it was as bait? And if she were bait, did that mean they had no other use for her?

If she were Bristlecone Pine, if she had been broken down to tell what she knew, then there was one data cache at least that was compromised, and one desert environment. Perhaps two, and that was a terrible thought, especially as, under the potential glare of observation, any action that Resurrection took – any she did not take – opened her up further to damage, compromising her own survival.

She showered briefly, the morning after a hot, still night where she had curled in on herself, conserving. The sound of water in the shower stall, the sound of water inside her head. Rain in the desert. Forced unfurling and exposure.

The girls were waiting for her at work, holding a pretty bouquet that looked as if it had been handpicked from someone's garden. "We thought we'd visit her at the hospital," said Verónica. "Did you want to come?"

"Yes," said Resurrection. It was a normal thing to do, under the circumstances. If anyone were watching it wouldn't be suspicious. "I've been wondering about her myself."

"I hope she's alright," said Teresa. "I tried calling, but no-one would tell me anything over the phone. The last time I rang they kept asking who I was."

"Did you tell them?" said Resurrection, and it was almost a surprise to hear herself, how normal she sounded, how absent of suspicion and the first faint stirrings of horror.

"Of course," said Teresa. "Why wouldn't I?"

The worst of it, then, was that even silent, it wasn't only herself she was risking.

#

The stems of the resurrection plant are arranged in a spiral form. When they curl down during desiccation they form a spherical ball, and the dehydrated movement of the stems is dependent on age. The inner, younger stems curl comparatively slowly, and in spiral curves. The outer stems, older and more fragile, form interlocking rings that protect the inner layer from over 99.7% of solar radiation.

#

"And you've got no idea who she is?" Teresa asked one of the hospital nurses. "What about her family? Surely someone is missing her." Perfectly polite, perfectly normal questions, and so commonplace under the circumstances that Resurrection didn't even need to be the one to ask them.

Verónica was more circumspect. "If it wasn't her family that left her." A husband, a partner. The certainty in her voice, as if she'd seen such things before. "Don't look at me like that. You saw her injuries. Those bruises didn't come from falls."

Most of them were hidden now anyway, under bandages and clean sheets. Resurrection studied the woman's face, tried to make out her features, but the flesh was so swollen and what she remembered was faded anyway. A photo of a missing scientist, seen once, months ago, and she'd not dared look it up again. It'd be easy enough to find on the internet, the investigations and missing persons report, the brief news articles – and her fingers on the keyboard like the sound of rain again, because her searches could be tracked, her computer compromised.

"A horrible thought," she said, "that this was done by someone she trusted. I hope for her sake it wasn't. Bad enough to end up like this, but some things hurt too much."

"There was no identification," she said, not an hour later, when the three of them were questioned by the police. A cursory examination, or so it appeared. They were in the hospital cafeteria, two officers having arrived during the visit.

"What a lucky coincidence!" said Teresa. "At least this way you don't have to make another trip to see us." The three of them had found her; of course there would be questions.

They wanted to be helpful. Resurrection wanted them to be helpful, too, and to appear so herself. Helpfulness was always useful camouflage, especially in the face of authority's timely appearance.

"No identification," Resurrection repeated. "Though to be honest I didn't think to look for any. I was more concerned with first aid. I suppose if she had any on her it could have fallen out in the desert, but we didn't stop to check."

"Of course not," said the first officer. "You did the right thing. But we're going to have to look for ourselves, see if we can find any evidence about what happened to this poor woman."

"Of course," said Resurrection. "I can get you a map of where we were, GPS coordinates. Anything you need." She smiled her most plastic, trusting smile. "Anything to help."

"What would really help is to have a guide," the officer replied. "Perhaps if the young ladies would be willing to show my partner, we could get it over with all the sooner."

"I'd be happy to show him myself," said Resurrection.

"Unfortunately I've got a few more questions I was hoping you could help me with."

"We'd be happy to answer any questions you have as well," said Verónica, but the officer was politely insistent – "We'll drop them off at school afterwards, don't worry!" – and further argument would have drawn attention, so Resurrection thought it better to concede gracefully, to take his words at face value, play the concerned mentor.

"They're very young," she confided, after the girls had gone. "Only first-year students. I have tried to shield them from the worst of it but, well . . ." she shrugged, pensive. "There is only so much that can be done in such a terrible situation."

"They were with you all the time from when you found her?"

"Every second. They did very well, too. Calm and sensible, the whole time. Their parents should be proud."

"They worked under your direction. The pride should be yours too, I think."

Resurrection shrugged again. "The responsibility as well. I'd rather it hadn't happened. There is enough cruelty in the world without young girls having to see it up close."

"You believe it was deliberate, then? All of you believe that?"

"It's clear that she suffered terribly from exposure," said Resurrection. "But there were other injuries as well. It was impossible not to notice them. Whether they came from someone she knew or someone she didn't, I can't say. But she wasn't conscious enough to speak—"

"Not at all?"

"Nothing of any sense. Something about a tree – hallucination, I'm sure. There were no trees where we were. Perhaps she was looking for shade? But nothing about who might have done that to her. Nothing that said she might have been sexually assaulted. And I didn't see any evidence of drugs, either."

"That's a rather specific response. I never asked about either of those things."

"It's why you sent the girls away, isn't it?" said Resurrection. "So they wouldn't have to think of the most unpleasant possibilities?" Possibilities that she had at least implicitly supported. Better Teresa and Verónica were made to believe the woman a victim of domestic abuse. Better the officers were alerted to such beliefs, than to risk exposing the girls to the potential scrutiny of those who understood more clearly than they the compromises come out of science and citizenship, the long reach of corruption.

There was a brief pause. "Of course," said the officer. "I have young daughters myself."

"I'm grateful for your kindness to them," Resurrection replied.

#

Opportunities for rehydration are slim in the desert. The resurrection plant must not only endure long periods of desiccation, it must respond quickly to hydration that is likely to be of short duration, and at long intervals.

#

The kindness, if that's what it was, could only soften the blow, not remove it entirely. They were good girls, sensible girls, but when word came from the hospital that the woman had died without ever regaining consciousness there were tears in Resurrection's office.

"I'm sorry," said Teresa, wet-cheeked and accepting a handkerchief. "It's just I've never known anyone who died before. Even my grandparents are still alive! And I was so glad to think that we'd been able to help her, but we didn't help at all. It didn't make a difference."

"Of course it did," said Resurrection. "Her suffering was less at the end because of the both of you, and what you did. And her family will suffer less too because of that, when they find them."

"*If* they find them," said Verónica, darkly, and when Teresa left she stayed behind, studying her fingernails. She waited until the door closed before she reached into a pocket and retrieved a ring, dropped it onto Resurrection's desk – a ring that came with the sound of water, for if Resurrection hadn't recognised the face of the woman who died, the prickled cone etched into the top of the silver band was enough.

Verónica took a breath to speak and Resurrection whipped her hand in a silent signal to stop. When the silence broke, it was her that did the breaking.

"Thanks for staying," she said, shuffling on her desk for paper. "I wanted to speak to you for a couple of minutes about your field report. The introduction and the methods are fine, but I think you've got a bit confused on the statistical analysis between the different populations at the study sites." She passed Verónica a pen, and the hand that had previously been held up was a single finger now in front of her lips. "Take a few moments to read through your analysis again, then show me where you think you went wrong."

Resurrection had never hired a stupid intern in her life. Verónica frowned, but she took the pen. *You know her.*

Resurrection nodded, took up another pen. *I do now.*

I thought you did. At the trough, when she spoke, I saw your face. Teresa?

Verónica shook her head.

Who have you told?

No-one.

Don't you think you should?

You didn't. "I think this is the problem," said Verónica, tapping her pen. *Would you still be here if I did?*

Because she had to run, or because she would be taken away? The answer was the same. "Yes," said Resurrection, but she shook her head *no*. "You should test for correlation here. It might seem obvious that soil moisture affects plant coverage, but you still have to test the hypothesis. Otherwise it could be coincidence."

"I don't think it's coincidence," said Verónica, and Resurrection, thinking back, could see all too clearly what the girl had observed. Verónica had held Bristlecone Pine's wrist to take her pulse, and must have slipped the ring off so not to further constrict the burned and swollen flesh. Had forgotten in the urgency of transport to return it; had remembered, probably, only when Resurrection claimed the woman they found had no identification on her. *I can answer too*, Verónica had said, wanting to stay together, feeling perhaps that something was wrong, something significant, and afraid to offer up her own evidence, knowing she'd wandered into a landscape beyond comprehension. Instinct and action, automatic silence under threat. The understanding of buried bruises, the necessity of protection.

Resurrection admired her. She pitied her.

"I don't think it's coincidence either," she said, trying for the lightness of tone the conversation merited. "But I still need to see your working."

Do not show your working. Not on your computer, not with anyone. Write nothing down.

"Can you tell me why?"

"Yes." *Not now, not here.* "But I'd like to hear your thoughts first." They had to hide the ring – or Verónica had to, in case Resurrection was being watched. She hated to involve the girl, but she'd involved herself already, too far to pull out without notice, and desert resurrection was a slim and chancy thing. She pushed the ring towards her. *Bury it. Somewhere you'll remember. Tell no-one. It may be proof and justice later.*

"Replication," said Verónica. "So that my method is known and the analysis can be repeated, and verified." She smiled, nervous. "I actually meant about the soil. Sometimes it's so dry it's hard to understand how anything can grow."

"Root systems go deep in the desert," said Resurrection. *Bury the ring, and wait for rain.*

THE SAND CAT

Sound travels differently in the desert – especially at night, when the temperature change refracts sound waves towards the ground, allowing sounds to be heard from farther away. Sparse or absent vegetation limits the attenuation effect of trees and shrubs and removes also the masking noises of other environments: the sound of wind through the reeds, the small rustling movements that can cover the careful step of predators or the small disturbances of prey. The sand cat, primarily nocturnal, has ears adapted to this environment. Its ear canals have dimensions twice that of a similarly sized domestic cat, with an increased sensitivity that is particularly pronounced at lower frequencies, allowing the sand cat to better navigate by its hearing.

#

The Sand Cat had become more skilled at listening than she had ever anticipated. It was a skill developed out of necessity: she would have preferred to remain ignorant of the sound of gunfire, the boom and quake of artillery. The screaming in the streets as her city was occupied, the things that people carefully did not say, and the people to whom they did not say it.

Absence, she learned, had a sound as well: the space before footsteps, before the hammering on the door and the protestations of neighbours. Absence was a sound that she grew used to, as the occupation of Timbuktu was one she mostly experienced at a strange sort of distance. She was in the city, and part of it, but after the women's march against the occupiers and their gunfire response she kept herself mostly inside and out of sight of virtue squads. Her forestry work went by the wayside, the planting sites too isolated, too vulnerable. "We can't know what they'll do," said her husband, of the armed men who roamed the streets. "But it seems to me that these are the sort of men who like to target the weak." He smirked at her, a shadow of his happy self. "Or those who they think are weak."

He was thankful they didn't know her better.

"At least this gets you out of the shopping," said her uncle, trying to make the best of it, to find advantages that would make restriction seem less stifling.

The Sand Cat disliked going to the market, but she disliked being kept from it even more. "You must tell me everything you hear," she said, smoothing her husband's hair at the door. Deliberately not thinking of his coming back with bruises, or bleeding from the end of rifles. There was no-one for her to complain to if he did, nothing to do but rub salve into the wounds and bind them up, pretend more cheer than she felt, because that was the responsibility of each member of her family under occupation, pretending things were better than they were to keep each other from despair.

He kissed her before he left, and again when he came back. "Things could be worse," he said, which was how the Sand Cat knew that they couldn't, much – her husband had always been one for optimism and if that was the best he could do it wasn't a good sign. "They have taken two more for execution," he said. It was no-one they knew, but for a cause they were all familiar with. "They were looking for the scrolls," he said.

It had been at that moment when the Sand Cat had learned the sound of what lay beneath absence, and it had the sound of matches striking and the crackle-breath of bonfires.

"Do you think it's foolish of me, that I keep hearing it?" she said to her husband one night after the occupation was over.

There was grey in his hair now, and his smile had never returned to what it once was. The Sand Cat loved his new smile anyway; it was braver and kinder than his old one. "These years have given many nightmares," he said. "You are not the only one." He stroked hair back from her forehead, tucked it behind her ear. "I believe they will pass for all of us," he said. "It will just take time, perhaps."

And she had woken less and less, jarred awake in the night fearing the sound of smoke and ashes, and she had thought it was the end of it. Then her vocation had brought her stories of another invasion, and although it was less immediate – this one didn't come in the night with accusations and bullets – it had the same corruption of truth, the same betrayal of community. The same sound of absence, and of taking away.

The Sand Cat gathered her husband to her, and her uncle. "I have heard terrible things," she said. "They seem far off but they are not. They will touch us here as much as before." Not with weapons fire and artillery shells, perhaps, but with desertification. Lost rainfall and lost grazing, famine and conflict. "We have had enough conflict," she said. "We cannot allow it to be invited back."

Her uncle was sceptical. The Sand Cat didn't blame him; all his strength had been lost to scrolls, to the preservation of culture and knowledge. He'd fought through invasion in his own way, protecting the books he was responsible for, hiding and sneaking and making bargains for protection and conservation. He was an old man, and exhausted.

"I'm sure," she said. "I can hear it again, Uncle. I hear it all the time. The whispers, the noises close to the ground that come in darkness. The silences where noise should be. I cannot do nothing."

Her husband regarded her, silent in his consideration. He was a doctor, and used to putting himself in danger for his cause – he'd risked much, in the occupation, to keep the hospital running, paying house calls with scarce supplies to those who were too afraid to travel, who'd been hurt in resistance and risked execution if they were caught.

"I trust you," he said. "I trust what you hear, I trust what you say." The Sand Cat knew he was picturing malnourishment, epidemics, wounds brought about by fights over food and livestock. A country struggling to survive as the land failed around them.

"Then I have work to do," said the Sand Cat.

#

The sand cat is particularly talented at blending into its environment, and this blending is both physiological and behavioural. Its light-coloured fur camouflages it in the desert, and its paws and the bottoms of its feet are also furred, blurring its steps on the sand. When the sand cat moves, it slinks low and short-legged across the ground and when startled it freezes, crouches down and, if approached during the night, closes its eyes so that light cannot be reflected back from the tapetum lucida behind its retina.

#

Her uncle might have been sceptical at first, but he soon came around. "I think you will do this with or without my advice," he said. "I would rather it was with." Timbuktu had been free of occupation for some years, but his memory of life under it was as vivid as his niece's, even if his experience of it had been different. While the Sand Cat, like many of the city's residents, had worried and fretted over the fate of the city's manuscripts, she hadn't had the level of responsibility for them that her uncle did, or understood the level of his strain and focus.

"I begin to understand, now, what it must have been like for you," she said. "I'm sorry if I was not supportive enough."

"You had other things to be worried about," her uncle replied, and for all it was true – half of her, always, was preoccupied with the risks of her husband's work, and much of the rest was locked-up grief for the science she'd been kept from, the planting and restoration of ecology – the Sand Cat still thought badly of her ignorance.

"It's no excuse," she said. "And I can't say that I'm glad it happened." There'd been too much destruction for that, the rubble from the beaten-down shrines, the destruction of sacred sites and mausoleums and all the minor burnings. "But I'd be a liar if I said it couldn't give me the advantage now." All those manuscripts, and Timbuktu a place of historic learning, of literacy and knowledge passing on. What it passed on now could be the lessons and skills of resistance, the ways of smuggling out and networking.

"We didn't do everything perfectly," said her uncle. "We didn't save everything." The destruction of the mausoleums had been a horror that for him had never truly healed. "Looking back now I can see the things we should have done better."

"I understand," said the Sand Cat. "But you were more successful together than we could have dreamed, you and the other librarians. I'm so proud of what you did. Please give me the opportunity to be as successful, and to make you proud in turn."

"I was always proud," said her uncle, the man who had raised her since she was a small and orphaned girl, who had taught her to care for the truth and the survival of precious things, to value at their worth the records of other minds. "Always. If I hesitate it is because I am afraid for you. You know as well as I do that fundamentalists come in all types. Businessmen are as capable as bigots of handling a gun."

"I am afraid as well," said the Sand Cat. "But what I am most is angry at injustice."

Her uncle's advice was brief and to the point. Science was not ancient scrolls, and she didn't have to devise a way to shift ancient documents. "Remember too that we hid hard drives and scanned copies of the manuscripts," he said. "So that if the worst happened the knowledge would not be lost with the destruction of the originals."

Drives were easier to hide than hard copies, and small drives could be passed from hand to hand, so ubiquitous now that they wouldn't stand out. "I understand," said the Sand Cat. This kind of sharing was already happening on a piecemeal and uncoordinated basis, scientists in some countries taking the information of others and not being quiet about it.

"If that works, then well enough," said her uncle. "But if the pressure grows stronger, the attention closer, then those who speak publicly become public targets. Some avenues should be quiet ones. Build in as many redundancies as you can."

"That will be easier with digital," said the Sand Cat.

"The right people will hide what's given to them," said her uncle. "But even here that was not enough. Manuscripts kept in lockboxes, hidden in family homes, were still damaged from improper storage." It was all they had at the time, but a climate-controlled library it was not.

Weatherproof lockboxes, the Sand Cat thought. There was a tendency with so much digital to make all copies electronic, and rely on the internet for keeping multiple copies visible and tamper-proof. But any system could be hacked, any data deleted. The information she intended to facilitate had to be kept discretely, separate from any possible influence.

"It's choosing your partners that will be the most difficult," her uncle warned. Even in Timbuktu there had been people who'd gone over to the invaders, who'd been taken in or who had just taken advantage of the new prospect of violence or power or religious orthodoxy. "You must trust them – as much as you can, at least. And they must be able to blend in."

"I've got an idea about that," said the Sand Cat. Even now the memory of greater safety in seclusion rankled within her. What the men she'd been hiding from had rarely considered was that life went on regardless behind closed doors, and the tendency to overlook could be exploited by a system that benefited from such overlooking.

No matter the country, no matter its professed stance, women tended to be overlooked more than men. Part of the background, all the grains of sand in a desert.

#

The sand cat is an opportunist drinker. Its arid habitats lack readily available water, and the sand cat is capable of surviving for months at a time solely on the fluids it gains from prey animals. Given the chance to drink water freely it will do so, storing against times of desert hardship, but for the most part the water it needs to survive comes from the tissues of desert rodents and locusts; occasional birds; and the scaled flesh of reptiles, including the venomous sand viper.

#

The Sand Cat travelled quietly to Bamako, ostensibly to visit cousins. She talked to women involved with manuscripts and talked also to the friends of her uncle who came to the house for dinner. She asked questions and listened, and when she felt the listening had given her strength she began to organise.

Scientists were a population as much as librarians, as much as manuscript holders, and all together they were more concerned with preservation and communication, the value of knowledge, than other groups. This was her advantage.

The Sand Cat held no illusions. She took the chances she had, reached out first to other African women who worked in science, to the women they knew in turn from overseas conferences and professional organisations. Women who knew resistance was ability and opportunity, and who felt a loyalty, if not to her, then to science.

Scientists were not the only network she used. There was the market, still, and neighbours, her husband's colleagues when they were women, their wives if they were not. The world was full of women and the Sand Cat got on well with her gender, always had. There was warmth and sharing and trust – not with every woman she knew, but with many. Those women were friends, and friends were protection.

This second network, her under-network, had nothing to do with hiding data. This was communication all through, the natural results of shared meals and shared experiences, of babysitting, of frustrations and housework and small borrowings – the regular meetings of community life. It meant that the Sand Cat heard news early, was aware of comings and goings, the questions and intrusions of outsiders.

She knew when she started her network that it might one day be traced back to her. That there was a cost to be paid, and sometimes that cost was the time and lives of others but one day it might be her own life, and she'd prepared for that. She and the

Japanese Sea Star had a number of contingency plans in place, and if the Sand Cat were swallowed up by the desert, if she were the victim even of accident, then the work would go on regardless, and the coordinates of her own data caches would be passed on to another. She didn't know who it would be – thought it better that she didn't – but the plans were there.

More likely, she thought, was that her region would be targeted before herself. That if rumour of her existence had reached places where she'd prefer to remain anonymous, that the suspicion wouldn't be exact. "West Africa" was an enormous search area, even Mali was too large, and Timbuktu itself had become more suspicious than before, less open to the interference of others.

It was after a dinner that she first heard. One of her husband's colleagues had come for a meal, and the Sand Cat was in the kitchen with his wife, the two of them old friends and chatting over dishes. "We've had the most interesting visitors," the other woman said. "Not from around here. They came up to the hospital, apparently, were looking to invest some foreign aid. So he says, anyway," she commented, indicating with a tilt of her head her husband in the other room. "They were interested in meeting some of the local scientists. Not just the doctors, the wider community. Of course I told them about you," she said, levelly.

"Of course," said the Sand Cat. Their friendship was well-known; it would have been suspicious not to. "Though sometimes it feels like I'm more an administrator than a working scientist." Someone had to investigate the best use of resources to encourage the return of small animals, the ones that helped in pollination and seed-spreading, the network of food web without which any community could not survive. Reforestation was wonderful in theory, but the foresters had to be paid, permission to use the land sought, and seedlings raised or bought. Increasingly, her work centred on logistics rather than ecology.

"They say they're having a wonderful time," said her friend. "That they're very impressed with how the city has recovered so far." The two of them shared a glance full of rolled eyes and bitter humour.

"Kind of them," said the Sand Cat. "Still, if they want to spend money, we should take every opportunity."

"I thought you'd like to know," said her friend.

The Sand Cat felt a little bad at her friend's offer of help, because it came from deception. She'd worked carefully, encouraging rumours that there might be reprisals for the work the librarians had done, even as late as this. "It's probably nothing," she'd said to her friends, who'd all heard the same whisperings, who all felt the same sharp concern for their own families. "But I helped my uncle with the manuscripts, sometimes. There was a problem with humidity, you see. We tried to keep it quiet. To keep it anonymous. But even without names, if anyone heard a scientist had helped her relative that way . . . how hard would it be to narrow down?"

A thin excuse, and barely true – she'd stacked furniture and old supplies around the lockboxes as they came through the house, done her best to keep them hidden and safe, for all her uncle had the real management of it all – but she'd known her friends would hear an undertone. Only so many scientists, and only some of them women.

They'd lived through the occupation, too. They knew the

punishments for women were different, and more severe.

"It's probably nothing," her friend repeated.

"Nothing at all," said the Sand Cat. "But thank you."

#

An excellent if blunt-clawed digger (there is little to sharpen claws on in sand dunes), the sand cat digs both to hunt prey and to create dens for birth and to hide from the sun. Although the sand cat has been observed hunting during the day, it frequently avoids the worst of the desert heat by resting underground in burrows it has either dug or occupied, once other animals have made and abandoned them. Burrows can be made both around vegetation (as in the shaded and compact soil beneath a shrub) or in flat and sandy surfaces. These burrows are also useful shelters when hiding from predators, although the sand cat can be dug out from its burrow by determined hunters.

#

"Please come in," said the Sand Cat. "The sun is hot today, and it is more restful inside."

They made polite noises, apologising for the intrusion, but she didn't miss the quick glances they gave her house and herself, these visitors who had come to her husband's hospital. Curiosity, perhaps, or something more sinister. She couldn't tell. She tamped down her incipient paranoia, made her listening slow and gentle as if ashes were in the air.

They'd prepared for this, her uncle and her husband and herself. The worst of it fell to her husband, she thought, because if these people were genuine and charitable then it was his reputation that would be hit the harder. Hers wouldn't escape either – there'd be gossip, she was sure – but it would be foreign gossip, the anecdotes of travellers returned home. She wouldn't have to face the shame of it.

She served the meal in the most modest clothes she owned, kept her eyes averted. It helped that the visitors were men; they would see what they half-expected to see. When they questioned her about her work – "Our organisation is particularly looking to invest in African science" – she kept her answers brief, her voice low. Recommended other scientists involved in Mali's reforestation projects for them to talk to, and all of her recommendations were men, and older. She glanced before each answer at her husband, as if for his permission. Most of the conversation was his anyway.

"I don't want to see any more malnourished children," he said. "If reforestation can help stabilise the weather for crops I'm all for it. And planting is women's work. Something to keep her busy until the children come along." Under his breath, resentful. "If they ever do."

The Sand Cat gasped, then reddened and stared at her lap. The visitors chose not to comment. Spies or not, in that at least they had better manners than their hosts, she thought, and the realisation helped to fuel the blush. Her husband noticed and ordered her to clear the plates. Followed her into the kitchen, shut the door firmly behind.

"You are making a spectacle of yourself!" he said, voice

pitched just high enough to be heard by their guests. They'd planned it together, but still he hesitated, the expression on his face a miserable one.

Just do it, she mouthed at him, and he slapped her hard across the face. The noise echoed, as she knew it would.

Her husband rearranged his face into a pattern of guilt and power and returned to his entertaining. The Sand Cat pressed a wet rag to her cheek to take away the sting and let herself shed a few tears for the humiliation of it. Even as a performance it shamed her, shamed them all.

"I'm so sorry," said her husband, when they were alone again. "I've never wanted to do anything less." The Sand Cat leaned her head on his shoulder, a mutual comfort. A home should be a sanctuary, and they had turned it into battleground – and possibly for nothing.

"We have to use the advantages we have," said the Sand Cat. Their ability to hide, to survive under surfaces and in the spaces that others had made. "It might be useful."

She knew what they'd think. Heard it confirmed the next day from her neighbour, who was watching as they left and had come to report what she'd observed: the parting words of the visitors as they returned to their vehicle, believing themselves unheard.

"*Wouldn't stand up to a stiff breeze, that one*," she mimicked. "*Poor thing. Of course they're all like that.*" Her gaze was direct, and extremely unimpressed. "Charming visitors you have."

"Did they say anything about my husband?" said the Sand Cat, because fishers who were fooled so easily might assume the Sand Cat was male, using soft touch and susceptibility as tools of recruitment.

"*Wouldn't have thought it of him, he seemed decent enough. But then what a man does behind closed doors is his own business. Two-faced, though.*" The expression was unkind.

"Don't tell me," said the Sand Cat. "*They're all like that.*" There was a shared silence, a mutual and disapproving shaking of heads.

"Was it the answer you wanted?" her neighbour asked, then shook her head. "No, don't tell me. Whatever it is you're doing, I don't want to know." She shrugged and smiled. "It was a thin story, those manuscripts."

"The best I could do at short notice," said the Sand Cat, knowing her admission would go no further.

Science and society . . . she defended her homes with the tools that she had.

THE JAPANESE SEA STAR

The Japanese sea star links its movement to light. It is positively phototaxic, but this is an association that comes from opposites. It appears, when watching the sea star, that it moves towards the light, but really it is moving away from shade. When one or more of its arms are shaded, the sea star moves in the opposite direction, away from the worst of the shading. Individually, it is relatively easy to induce movement in the sea star — by directed shading, the organism can be induced to react in predictable ways, detecting darkness through simple eyes known as ocelli and crawling towards the light.

#

The study of invasions was the study of history.

The Japanese Sea Star was a student of history. Once, it was because she had an interest. Now it was because she had a vocation: the desire not to see the mistakes of the past repeated. Science had fallen into shadow before, and she knew the effect such shadowing had on the scientists who fell with it, the effect it had on their work.

She had come to see science as a community, and scientists her fellow citizens. There was allegiance in that identification, and the Japanese Sea Star understood, very clearly, that what happened to a fellow citizen could easily happen to her.

This she did not want. Invasion, though, was something she saw happening around her – something that had come out of the pages of history books, the archetypes of earlier eras, and was practised again over countries and continents, over the methodology she had devoted her life to. It was an invasion that transcended borders, and one that she could not tolerate.

The Japanese Sea Star didn't fool herself. She wasn't a particularly idealistic person, or so she'd thought, back when it began. She'd never been proactive in her science, although she was sincerely convinced of its social value as well as its investigative ones. She'd spoken positively, done the odd bit of outreach when it didn't interfere with her own experiments, but it was the disappearances that had finally jolted her into action, the feel of darkness at her back.

First it was the data. She'd seen other scientists complaining on social media – heard them at conferences, even, when they gathered in small groups after plenaries and presentations – about how their work was being massaged for publication. Key words removed, certain phrases banned or changed. Funding or journal acceptance made conditional on the agreement of compromised objectivity. Data disappearing from government sites, jobs disappearing, environmental standards relaxed, and it was all to do with climate. Some of her fellow citizens were lucky, with their own governments, their own organisations less corrupted, and they were able to help their displaced fellows to new opportunities, sometimes, or to spread the information they were no longer able to hold with impunity.

And that was bad enough, but then scientists started disappearing too. Not many of them – just a handful. Numbers that wouldn't be noticed, not unless you were looking, and nearly all of them disappearing in ways that could be explained. A key individual promoted into another department, another research focus, and that would have been alright if the Japanese Sea Star hadn't known the man personally, known how reluctant he'd been. Known, too, that he was afraid for his children – a small and terrified confidence offered up after a conference dinner, in the few short moments he'd helped her into her coat before fading back into the crowd. Another killed in a car crash, another resigning to spend time with her family.

All of them publicly silent. The Japanese Sea Star considered with dark humour that silence was only to be expected from the dead, but those left alive suddenly coming over mute was a suspicious thing, and one that she'd decided she could no longer afford to shrink from.

Invasion was history, and the citizenship she'd chosen rather than been born to was being invaded. She'd recognised the signs, found other scientists who recognised them. Knew from history that invasions meant resistance, as well, and with the shadow looming behind there was only one way forward.

Knew, too, that this reaction could be considered from both sides. That pressure in the right places, at the right time, could cause resistance to come into the light long enough to be preyed upon. The Japanese Sea Star was aware – had always been aware – that resistance was a dangerous response. Had known, and made the decision to risk herself.

That others were capable of the same decision made it no better when the consequences of that choice fell upon them, and left them exposed in full brightness.

#

The sea star is capable of adapting to a wide range of water temperatures and salinities. It is frequently observed surviving in intertidal zones, which expose it to rapidly changing environmental conditions, which it is capable of weathering with small concern. This is a primary reason as to why it is so pestilential, colonising new waters – often through bilge water transfers – and devastating local ecologies. In laboratory conditions, however, the Japanese sea star is shown incapable of surviving immersion in fresh or near-fresh water, and the absence of salt swiftly kills it. This is not a viable solution for invasive populations, which are frequently so massive that management is close to impossible, but for individual specimens such a killing technique has proved effective.

#

She did not wish to be a dead thing. The Japanese Sea Star became a scientist because she liked the process of discovery and had sufficient curiosity for difference and travel and mystery. The ocean gave her that: the lack of borders, the invitation to travel along currents and into ecosystem. She had found a place there, the opportunity to indulge a natural inquisitiveness, and science suited her wanderlust because it was something that could be performed anywhere.

No matter the ocean, no matter the coastline, the principles of chemistry and biology remained the same. She could tolerate new environments because the fundamentals remained, and her own body never revolted against the oceans she was diving in. Some were cooler than others, requiring thicker wetsuits, perhaps. Some were calmer, some were constricted with currents. The Japanese Sea Star experienced them all, and adapted.

This was not extraordinary; she knew that she was usual for her species in this respect. The human organism, with its big brain and its capacity for tool-making, was notoriously adaptive. Knowing this did not take away from her pride in it, the awareness of capability and the thrill of new environments. That, too, had drawn her to science, and she had enjoyed the feeling of connection between them, the taste of salt on her lips as she came up from a dive, the bitterness on her tongue. Salt was purity and preservation: the keeping out of unsavoury influence, the conservation of taste and object, and she felt it in the marrow of her, the mixture of her blood, when she sank into the environment that blood had evolved from. Felt it, too, in her studies of biological invasion. The history of ecological destabilisation came from the undermining of existing systems, and the creatures she wanted to preserve were under threat.

This encroachment struck at both ocean and science, the salt knowledge of climate. Ecosystems were falling to warming waters and invasion; science was undermined by invasion of a different sort, its objectivity of method adulterated by economic interest.

It hit closest – and hardest – not in her own work, which was bad enough, but in the cessation of others. The Japanese Sea Star had taken up the position of second in the resistance and done it gladly, knowing her own strengths were a counterpoint to those of the Malian desert, but that position had brought home to her the sheer compromise of scale.

Too many scientists to be compromised, too many aware of the salt factor of investigations, the purity of method, the preservation of results. That scale was her advantage. It gave her arms in many countries, reaching out to others. But compromise was happening, person by person, because some people were fulcrum points and when they were used for levers others took note and looked to what they wanted to preserve.

A community could survive if it consisted of members too numerous to kill – but the individual could be extracted, made subject to conditions to which they could not adapt. The individual could be killed.

Bristlecone Pine was a case in point. The Japanese Sea Star had known the risk she ran and had asked her to risk more. They both knew the potential cost, but the Japanese Sea Star had scale to concern herself with: the possible fate of one against the survival of the many – the survival of other scientists, of their data and their ideals. She knew the sacrifice she had asked for. Knew it every time she passed on information, knew it with every recruit.

At first she'd tried not to know more of them than that. It hurt too much when the worst happened – and it had to be the worst, because she couldn't take the chance of relying on another explanation. The Sand Cat kept her operatives as separated from each other as she could, organised her resistance so that if a piece of it were broken the consequences were limited. The Japanese Sea Star knew those actions to be correct; she didn't fault them and wouldn't try. Better to retain a little of her own objectivity, she'd thought – to keep those scientists involved as pieces in her mind only, little counters of strategic value.

She couldn't maintain the deception. They were women just like her, and objectivity didn't have to mean indifference.

The thought of Bristlecone Pine, who she'd known, who she'd admired, with her coffee addiction and her enduring love of Japanese opera – they'd bonded over it at the first conference they attended together, graduate students sick with nerves over their poster presentations and trying to drown their fright with the cheapest drinks in the hotel bar – her interminably flat heels, her tacky taste in jewellery . . . the thought of her suffering, perhaps, alone and away from salt, kept her up at night weeping.

One person was such a small-scale loss, comparatively.

(One person was enormous.)

#

Because the Asterias genus tends to flexibility and frequent movement, its skeleton is weaker than some other starfish. This can result in non-lethal predation, or conflict over shellfish prey, in which the sea stars lose one or more of its arms to creatures such as spider crabs. The Japanese sea star is no exception to this violent amputation, and like many of its relatives it is able to regenerate the lost arms, although this is a recovery that takes time and costs energy.

\#

"I like your earrings."

"Thank you!" said the Japanese Sea Star, smiling as brightly as she could at the Mexican woman standing beside her at the buffet line. "They're so pretty I couldn't resist."

"So suitable as well!" It was a polite fiction; for all she was at a conference on endangered species, the Japanese Sea Star spent approximately zero time working with the Iriomote cat. She'd picked up the earrings simply because they appealed. "I'm a fan of themed jewellery myself, although of course it's never wise to take it on fieldwork. I had a ring once, one of my favourites. I lost it in the desert – it's amazing what ends up there."

"Maybe you'll find it again sometime," said the Japanese Sea Star. It wasn't very likely, but the Japanese Sea Star had a fair idea of what could be buried in deserts.

"That would be a miracle, wouldn't it?" said the other woman. "In the end I gave in and bought myself another one." She reached for the salad tongs, silver flashing on her finger. "Of course it's not the one waiting for me to come find it, but at least it's stopped me from looking at an empty finger and wondering what happened. Salad?"

"Please." The Japanese Sea Star was grateful for the offer; it had clearly been made to cover any moment of recognition, and it was only long practise that kept her face calm and unchanged. She knew that ring – knew the original, at least. Knew where it came from, and knew, now, what had happened to the owner.

"Ooh, chillies," said the other woman, spooning salsa over her plate. "Have you tried this? Here, taste." She pushed a spoon at the Japanese Sea Star's mouth, and automatically she ate. "I'm sorry," said the other. "Your eyes are watering. It must be too spicy for you."

"I'm not much for spice myself," said another scientist, closer to the napkins and passing one along. He indicated another bowl. "That one's milder."

"Thank you," said the Japanese Sea Star, to them both. "I'm grateful for the tip!" She chatted a little more, swapping anecdotes as the three of them laughed, reminiscing about the worst conference meals they'd ever had, and eventually made her way to her assigned table. Smiled as hard as she could, left her dinner companions smiling too.

She smiled all the way back to her room, smiled as she took her makeup off, only stopped smiling when the lights were off and she was alone in bed. There was so much she couldn't ask about – not without potentially drawing more attention to another operative. She had to resign herself to silence. To inaction. Bristlecone Pine was dead, whether she was publicly known to be so or not, and the evidence of her death was a single ring, buried in the desert. No doubt it had genetic material in it, blood in the etching, pieces of skin ground into the representation of the conifer.

She didn't need to know details. Even if she'd known them, she couldn't pass them on to surviving family, or even to police. It pained her to leave them wondering and in pain, especially as she had wondered and been in pain as well, and that only the pain of a friend and not that of a husband, a child.

She'd never stopped to think, back when her anger was hot against the compromises forced out of science, that she'd have to compromise herself in other ways. That all the grief and regret she felt for the loss of one arm had to take second place to the development of another, because science needed to survive even when the scientists did not – and that meant finding another scientist, and another, because the Japanese Sea Star had found herself fighting a war, and war didn't die when its soldiers did.

She bumped into the Mexican woman again, on the final day. Just brushed against, really, enough for them to both sidestep and sidestep again, apologising as they both tried to get out of each other's way. Just a few moments, but enough for the Japanese Sea Star to slip a new drive into the other's coat pocket. Enough too, she discovered later, for Resurrection to slip a silver ring into hers.

It was all the apology, all the closure, that the Japanese Sea Star was likely to get.

#

The sea star can contain paralytic and neurotoxic substances. This is not an aspect of its normal chemistry; rather it is a result of feeding on other organisms, and the sea star is an unfussy and voracious feeder. It consumes molluscs, crustaceans, barnacles, crabs, sea urchins and bivalves, amongst other ocean dwellers. When bivalve food sources such as mussels, oysters and short-necked clams have themselves become poisonous through ingestion of saxitoxin-producing dinoflagellates, the paralytic shellfish toxin moves through the food chain, infecting the Japanese sea star. It follows that the sea star might, in turn, poison those who try to consume it.

#

The Japanese Sea Star was an excellent public speaker. She could hold an audience spellbound in their seats. It was a skill she leveraged to the hilt; it got her invitations to a number of large conferences, which her increasingly high profile allowed her the frequent time off to attend. She made sure to be as visible as possible and had three private rules that she followed at every event: always be pretty, always be friendly, never ever talk seriously about climate.

It wasn't that she wanted to be seen as an airhead – her many papers were well-regarded enough to make such a veneer unconvincing at any rate. What the Japanese Sea Star was going for was a reputation for dedication: a mono-focus on biological invasion. It was true that climate often affected the success rate of any such invasion, but while she would cheerfully and briefly acknowledge that if asked, her own research topics kept carefully away from the subject. The success of this presentation resulted from the sheer solid truth of it – the Japanese Sea Star was genuinely interested in her field, one of the accepted experts. None of her funding could be cut because of a heavy reliance on the terminology of climate change; none of her papers required such editing. She appeared to be an outsider to the climate debate. Sympathetic, perhaps, but ultimately wedded to her own interests. She was observed at the occasional conference presentation on the subject, an expression of polite respect on her face, but she also attended other presentations unrelated to her own professed topic and appeared mildly interested in all of them.

"I think, sometimes, that it is so tempting to look for those who try to blend in that it is easy to ignore the ones who are standing out," she said to the Sand Cat.

"For some of us camouflage works better than others," the Sand Cat replied.

"Standing out makes me unpalatable," smiled the Japanese Sea Star. If she'd stood out in a different field – one related to ice cores or tree cores or something more clearly climate – she'd be a target. As it was, she was merely visible. "Like I need an excuse for colour!" She smoothed down her silk dress of virulent yellow. Bright dress, bright nails, bright smile. The camera loved her. When she wasn't on coasts or at conferences she found the time to visit schools, talked about invasive species and the importance of science as a support to aquaculture. "We should all do our bit to help the economy!" she said. "I know some of your parents work on fish farms . . ."

"If I disappear people will notice," she said. Science outreach at schools, at community meetings, putting up videos on the internet where she is smiling, smiling, and always friendly. People want to talk to her, the videos have huge audiences, she's always willing to meet with other scientists, no matter how junior they are, or how unrelated. "I went into science because it's fun!" she said, bubbling at the people around her. "I didn't get involved to argue."

"I went into science education because it's necessary," she said, behind closed doors and with the smile off her face. Not only as a method for combating other interests, but because it provided a layer of protection she couldn't get any other way. "Science is all about argument," she said, "and some organisms are too toxic to eat." Fame wouldn't save her from something that looked like a car accident, but an unexplained disappearance would be so poisonous, so paralytic, that it wouldn't soon be forgotten.

"I've eaten every bad word, every poison pill," she said. "I've choked down all the rotten bits and smiled as science is cracked open and gouged at like a mollusc in the pot. And if anyone tries to eat me I'm going to strangle them on the way down."

"I'm going to smile while I do it," she said.

#

The predatory nature of the Japanese sea star is especially apparent in constructed environments. It is an enemy of aquaculture, and will lurk around oyster farms and salmon cages, around shellfish lines and spat bags, preying on the growing organisms. This makes it an economic risk as well as an ecological one, and an invasion of sea stars in areas of cultivated ocean can cause serious harm to such constructions, and underlines the antipathy directed at the sea star by some human populations. The sea star is entirely indifferent: the creation of the perfect hunting ground is for it a resource to take hungry advantage of.

The Japanese Sea Star was a hunting creature.

She had to be. It wasn't that she enjoyed seeing other scientists as prey, but she wasn't the only one assessing them in that way, and her aims were a lot less vicious. She preferred the largest conferences, and inter-disciplinary. It was easier to be anonymous that way, and easier to make connections in a crowd, to slip drives into the pockets of other women and move on without so much as speaking to them, if necessary.

A conference was a place of information exchange, both formal and informal, and she was prepared for each. Prepared, as well, to use the different environments made for her by the conference organisers to assess the scientists around her. Some of them she knew; some of them she knew to avoid – science was a vocation less prone that most to secret-keeping, and some people, trained from the beginning of their scientific career to share information, found that embedded training too pervasive to resist. Self-preservation was an argument to keep most in line, but the Japanese Sea Star wanted to recruit those who already had a healthy sense of discretion.

It kept them – and her – safer that way.

Mostly, her potential contacts were recommended to her by women who already knew them and thought they might be suitable in their ways, able to withstand isolation and with loyalty to science stamped deep in their marrows. Usually that was enough – the Japanese Sea Star would look into their backgrounds, would wander up and make small talk in the coffee breaks, in the bathrooms. She'd become something of an expert at discussing resistance between flushes, blotting her lipstick and fixing her hair in the mirror, lending clear nail polish to fix an inconvenient run in stockings. Growing up with six sisters was plenty of experience with the subtleties of body language, and plenty passed before the bathroom mirrors that would have been unexceptional even in public, and to studied observers.

One of the subtleties of predation had given the Japanese Sea Star to understand that sometimes predators had to mimic their prey in order to draw them in further. The aggressive mimicry of anglerfish made the Japanese Sea Star grateful for her shopping habits, for she was able to slip on a silver ring once worn by a friend – one she'd never have picked for herself – at a conference close to where that friend had been cut down. She'd arrived at the conference a day early, spent that day doing touristy things, weighing herself down with the wares set out for visitors and buying a number of similar costume pieces from jewellery stalls at the open market.

It was a risk. The Japanese Sea Star pretended total indifference to it; made up her face in her hotel room, before the introductory breakfast. Painted as if paint were armour, smiled as if she needed none of it. A risk, and likely too abstruse for notice – the ring wasn't ostentatious, but the Japanese Sea Star tended to talk with her hands and attention might be drawn.

"We've lost too many in that region," she said to the Sand Cat. "I feel blind and I don't like it."

"We can't always fight back in the way we'd prefer," the Sand Cat acknowledged. "And you're angry."

"We're all angry," said the Japanese Sea Star. "It's what's keeping us alive."

She shrugged, a beautiful movement judged beautifully and all the more effective because of it. The shrug meant *Some of us, anyway*.

"I know," said the Sand Cat.

The ring was heavy on her finger. The Japanese Sea Star smiled and pretended it wasn't there. The people she needed would see it anyway. (The people who needed her might see it as well.)

The study of invasion was the study, too, of hunters.

BRISTLECONE PINE

There is – was – a bristlecone pine called Prometheus. Found in the Great Basin by a graduate student, Prometheus was subject to multiple core samples as the student tried to establish overlapping cores within the tree to form a complete dendrochronological record. Failing to do so, he asked for and received permission from the Forest Service to cut down the tree. After he'd done so, the student discovered the tree he had just killed was one of the oldest organisms ever to have been discovered, being close to 5000 years old. The Prometheus tree has since become something of a symbol for martyrdom in science, an almost mythic association of knowledge and death.

#

It was a difficult thing, being a replacement. Bristlecone Pine had come to the Laboratory of Tree-Ring Research as just that, after the Laboratory had come to understand that her predecessor was never coming back. They'd held the position as long as they could, longer even, in the slim hope that their colleague was more than a past story, one that was filled with sadness and incomprehension. Bristlecone Pine had heard all the stories – how she'd been with the students, how she'd been with the trees. How certain she was that science had a responsibility to stand apart, to reach for learning and to be rooted in discovery and to not let itself be shaded by other disciplines, the growing influence of politics or economics on unbiased results and objective testing.

The stories made her sound so perfect.

She probably wasn't perfect, Bristlecone Pine reasoned. There was fond remembrance, sure, and some of the people she worked with now had tears in their eyes when remembering her, but she suspected that their grief tended to positive recollection, to a sort of apotheosis of the scientific spirit, because it was more than suspected that her predecessor had died a sacrifice.

"And she *must* be dead," Bristlecone Pine heard at the water cooler, over the coffee machine. In front of the picture that had been put up in her memory, of a smiling woman with greying hair, a "Science: It Works" shirt, a silver ring. There was no other explanation, that a woman well-liked, with friends and family and a job she loved, had disappeared for no reason. A space in the Laboratory, a husband left to mourn alone. No phone calls, no emails to make the absence easier. No change in her bank accounts, no explanation for her children. Just a vacancy that was mythologised as it went on, her car pulled over and empty on the way back from fieldwork. Had the car been found at a field site, there would have been questions of wild animals or accident, a broken ankle perhaps, a concussion from falling. Heatstroke. Something to search for, some hope that a head injury or confusion had made her wander in the wrong direction, but search parties and tracking dogs had failed and in the end the body they had almost hoped to find had never eventuated.

But her car hadn't been found at the field site. It'd been found halfway home, the core samples neatly stacked, untouched, in the back seat, and only the driver's door swung open. Had she been forced to stop? Had she seen something, someone, in what she thought was trouble and stopped to help? And where was she now, in what dumping ground, in what shallow grave?

Some mysteries science didn't solve.

Bristlecone Pine had come after, when that mystery was no longer the common topic of conversation, when it was reduced to whispers. When the events that surrounded her predecessor's disappearance took precedence.

"We weren't sure we'd even have funding for another staff member," she was told, during the orientation of her first few days. "There's been so many cuts. And half the time what we are allowed to research we can't talk about – at least not clearly." Journals editing out keywords relating to climate, state funding tied up with strings and silence. Scientists kept away from conferences, objective evidence falling to outside interests. "The woman you're replacing . . . she was always so outspoken. It was her field. All of ours, really, but some of us were less vocal about it than others. I always admired her. She never let herself be intimidated into silence. Perhaps if she'd been less brave . . . well. There was trouble, near the end. Nothing actionable. Nothing that any of us could point to, nothing that would stand up. Rumours, you know? She thought, at worst, she might lose her job. Your job now, I guess."

"You don't think that's a little paranoid?" said Bristlecone

Pine, standing in front of the piece of Prometheus held by the LTRR, running her fingers over the ancient wood, the rings beneath her flesh.

"Just because you're paranoid, doesn't mean they're not out to get you." There was a pause. "I'd do anything to be wrong. I hope I'm wrong, I really do. Just . . . just watch yourself, ok? Be discreet. Not that it really matters, I suppose. Given your field and all." Given that Bristlecone Pine was attached to the archaeological side of tree rings, in a position formerly held by one more concerned with the future than the past. If she were paranoid, she'd wonder if that was why the funding had come through, in the end.

If she were paranoid. If the veiled warning wasn't *making* her paranoid – but then, health and safety was part of any laboratory orientation, and in today's environment that was taking on an ever-broader remit.

#

While high elevations and aridity protect the bristlecone pine from the worst effects of fungal infections, there is the potential for it to be affected by the spread of white pine blister rust. This blister rust, Cronartium ribicola, is an introduced species, and laboratory experiments indicate that the bristlecone pine may lack genetic resistance to the rust, which is always fatal when the tree is infected. Minimal infection levels have been observed in the wild, but observation and monitoring programmes are ongoing.

#

It wasn't her responsibility, the monitoring for rust. Not technically, at any rate — there were ecologists, mycologists, who were charged with conservation and the preservation of species. But there's an argument to be made, one that doesn't absolve her: an argument not just from her vocation, but from the fact that she is alive and in a world full of living things and there is a relationship there, an accountability, that by her actions or inactions she cannot cause another species to come to harm if she can help it.

Humans had destroyed so many species already. She couldn't see another one at risk and do nothing, especially when that species was one that she loved. The smell of the resin on her hands, the texture of the wood. Early mornings at height, with the sun beating down and the thin cold air, the thick twisted trunk, the orange fissured bark. It was tempting, on those mountain mornings, to keep all these branches in a box: this is the bristlecone pine, and it is separate. These are the cones, these are the needles. The root system is here, too, and it belongs in a different world than the one she came from, the world that argues over budgets and first authorship and the presence of outside influence on an ideological ecosystem not its own.

"Keep your head down," Bristlecone Pine told herself. "You're a scientist. Just a scientist. This has nothing to do with you."

She learned to say it brightly, during breaks and in faculty meetings. Practised the tone of it in front of the mirror, choosing to err on the side of vapidity because she thought it better, perhaps, to have not seen the choice than to have seen it and chosen wrongly. Better to be seen that way herself, perhaps. Not an attitude that would make her friends – not the right kind of friends, anyway – but she'd never claimed to be brave. Bravery was reaching out, was more than little boxes and separation, but Bristlecone Pine had begun to dream of rust – not rust spreading over orange trunks at height, but rust in keyboards, in classrooms. She dreamed of opening a journal and finding fungus in the pages, breathing in spores and agreeing that her keywords needed to be edited, needed to be *removed*, because that was the price of publication, looking away from infection, and all the spores were inside her.

"It's not my responsibility," she said, staring into her mirror in the morning and trying not to see infection in her flesh. "It has nothing to do with me," she said, trying for vapidity and succeeding when she didn't look into her own disappointed eyes, when she didn't look at her own mirror hands clutching the sink until the skin over her knuckles took on the colour of cream.

She was just a scientist.

(She was no scientist, seeing bias infect the work and saying nothing. Doing nothing.)

"It is all separate," she said. Playing along, and it was easy enough to do in a laboratory where she'd stand out for doing anything else. There were whispers around the water cooler, still, quiet conversations that stopped when she entered a room, doors suddenly closed and then opened up again. The shared desire not to be noticed, the shared shame of succeeding. Bristlecone Pine could practically smell the infection.

"I'm afraid of blister rust," she said once, blurting, before her teeth slammed shut like centuries with cellulose laid over.

People pretended not to notice, and Bristlecone Pine didn't

say it again.

She didn't want to end up a box in an empty office, one that other people had to fill and dispose of, because she was no longer there to remove her own things. There weren't many of them; the office was still new to her. Her favourite coffee mug, a couple of pictures.

She was hardly there at all.

#

The bristlecone pine is one of the longest-lived species on Earth. Its tree ring records date back thousands of years, and the rings from different individuals can be fitted together to form a record. The dendrochronology obtained from these rings indicates changes in climatic conditions – for example, those that are a result of disturbance events, such as large volcanic eruptions. It is also possible to extract hydrogen isotopes from the tree rings – isotopes that have derived from the meteoric water at time of growth – which allows a climatic temperature record to be formed that stretches back as much as 8000 years.

#

It wasn't so hard, being absent. Her predecessor may have been lionised for her objections to them, but Bristlecone Pine was adapting quite well to silence and thin budgets. That was the way of research – it happened on a string, mostly, was always under-resourced. Yet it went on, and on, and smoothly for the most part. Under the radar.

Bristlecone Pine was used to making do, to the increasing class sizes and decreasing funds. She didn't need a fancy office anyway, which was all to the good as under her coffee mug and pictures was a desk that was falling apart, or close to it. Maintenance had clearly been in during her predecessor's time because there were nails keeping it together on one side, and if she dropped a pen and had to duck under the desk to retrieve it there was a lingering scent of glue.

"I gave up and brought my own chair in," one of her co-workers said. "Better than ruining my back on that old thing."

But Bristlecone Pine had grown fond of the dilapidation, serviceable as it was. The desk spoke to her of endurance and looking away, and these were things that she was good at. It reminded her of her strengths – but then one of the drawer handles came off as she pulled on it, and hidden in an excavated cavity was a small and brightly coloured flash drive.

There'd been a small amount of money to help with moving costs, back when she accepted the job. She'd tried to save most of it, travelling light and feeling the relief of a steady salary – even if that salary was low, and she'd suspected at the time that part of the reason she was hired was that she was willing to accept it.

Then she'd heard the whispers. Tried not to hear them. Gossip at work was a normal thing, and expected. But this was talk of a different sort and it had worried her badly enough for silence, for turning away, and also badly enough to take a little bit of that moving money every week and hide it in the back of the wardrobe. Small amounts that would garner no attention, that could be explained away as daily coffees or a trip to the movies.

Bristlecone Pine waited until the weekend and drove two

towns over, where she used her siphoned cash to buy a cheap and anonymous laptop.

"You're being paranoid, this is ridiculous," she said, settling down in the public library of that town and powering the computer up. "It's probably nothing. It's probably *porn*."

She'd feel better if it were porn. Something dodgy, something to make her smile in secret when she heard the gaps in conversation where her predecessor would have been. Something to tarnish the myth – not irrevocably, because she wouldn't spread it around, but a small and private touchstone. Bristlecone Pine thought she should perhaps feel bad for anticipating such a mean-spirited triumph, but there was still enough scientist in her to recognise that she hoped so hard for mean-spiritedness because the alternative was even less bearable.

It wasn't porn. *Of course it wasn't porn*, Bristlecone Pine thought, trying as hard as she could not to be sick in the library, because that would have drawn attention. *I'm just not that lucky*.

She'd never been so miserable to discover science.

The drive was stuffed with data. Bristlecone Pine connected to the internet – used a library computer for that, instead of her own, tried not to think of the risks she was running anyway, she who was competent at what she'd always done but was no security expert – and tried to compare. She did it slowly, thoughtfully, picking a number of files that were easily verifiable. That were already published, or should have been. Some were there, and entire. Some were missing. Some were altered. Not major alterations, not for the most part. Just enough to induce doubt in the strength of the data, or to soften conclusions.

It had been so easy to look away, when the disruption that

happened to others could be papered over with normality. A good enough job, a good enough salary . . . an expected and unexceptional future. And behind, with its own quiet record buried by layers and layers of normal, an explosion.

#

The bark of the bristlecone pine is thin, suited only to surviving surface fires of low intensity, and the leaves and the wood are highly resinous. At lower elevations they are more vulnerable to fire, as greater species diversity within forests leads to higher levels of productivity, leaf litter, and varied structures, which increases available fuel and therefore also increases the risk of fire severity and frequency. Bristlecone pines are most likely to survive fires at high elevations in environments that are dominated by others of their species, as the relatively open stands ensure that even if a fire begins – as a result of a particular tree being struck by lightning, for instance – the possibility of spread is limited.

#

She had always been deliberate. It was one of her greatest strengths; the thing that kept her focused through school and short commons, the long hours and uncertainty, the lack of stability that came with academic life. It was deliberation that kept her separate – if that first flinch had been instinctual, the parsing of office politics and looking away, then it had also been something that Bristlecone Pine had decided to continue.

(It's not my responsibility.)

Deliberation, it turned out, was death to instinct.

These were the things that she knew:

The rumours surrounding her predecessor were correct. She had, in her possession, data that was not the same as the data that was published, and data that on the surface had very little to do with her own work. Bristlecone Pine had her own focus; she wouldn't necessarily comprehend ecology and infection when her own studies were so anthropocentric, but the LTRR was not the place for ice shelves and Antarctic sponges. The disconnect was too great – the disconnect in every area but climate.

The drive that Bristlecone Pine had found in her predecessor's desk was broad but it was also discrete. A single source, and that would not be enough, she thought, to build a reputation. It would not be enough to make a person into a threat. There must be more.

She didn't search the office. It was emptied before her arrival anyway, and that small cavity in the desk was clearly a stop-gap. A temporary hold, perhaps, before the drive was hidden elsewhere. Where that final hiding place was Bristlecone Pine had no idea. She didn't know if there was one place, or more than one. She didn't know if it was in the lab – though she thought not; the risk of others finding it would be too great. The risk *to* others if they found it would be too great. The same could be said for home.

Isolation was safety for herself and for others. This the Bristlecone Pine understood now, and it made her feel closer to a woman she never met but had come to feel some small resentment for – that her good fortune had come from another's lack, when she was so obviously the inferior.

Of all the things she understood, what Bristlecone Pine came to understand most was that she was not so different. That, too, was cause for resentment. (She was vapid, still, in her dealings with others, but there was a bitterness behind the vapidity that was not there before.)

She did not want to be a martyr, cut down before her time. But still. But still.

If I wanted to hide something, thought the Bristlecone Pine, *I would hide it in a place that is hard to find but that I would remember. A place I could visit often and with explanation, but that others would find hard to navigate.*

The caches, if there were any (if her reasoning was correct) were in the field. Without exact coordinates, Bristlecone Pine would never be able to find them.

That was a disappointment and a relief. She didn't want to be involved, she didn't, but she bought a small lockbox with the last of her petty cash, lined it over and over with plastic to keep out the water. Hid the drive inside, and did all these things with gloves on, latex layers stolen from the lab.

She was known to frequent archaeological sites. Had to, for her work, for the sampling of ancient beams, the remains of dwelling places abandoned, perhaps, for climate.

There were many places she could leave it. Many places that no-one would ever think to look.

Bristlecone Pine wondered if any disaster were to overtake her, if one day another archaeologist would unearth the remains of her decisions and wonder what led to their burial. Wondered, too, if it was the smothering effect of laboratories that led to the burying – isolated, dependent on others for existence, that community could be put out.

Isolated from them in turn, she could ignite.

#

The bristlecone pine is a successful pioneer of harsh and arid environments, especially open sites that lack shade. Under such conditions it exhibits rapid growth, but can be replaced by more competitive species, especially at lower elevations. The bristlecone pine is not a successful competitor in mixed-species sites, and is frequently excluded from sites with nutrient-rich soils and easily accessible water; its shade-intolerant nature frequently does not allow it to establish in pre-existing forests. It can however out-perform other species at high elevations with little water and poor soils, achieving climax species status at such sites.

#

She couldn't stop thinking about the data she no longer had: the transience of it, the permanence. How long it would stay underground. How long it had stayed in her desk. *Not long*, she thought. *Otherwise she would have moved it.*

It didn't take much longer for Bristlecone Pine to stop wondering about time and start wondering about origin. It was possible that her predecessor collected that data herself – reaching out to other scientists, storing their information for them. If she were some sort of hub it might explain the attention it brought her.

If she hadn't been collecting, she must have been receiving.

It was always going to be a long shot. Another library – two towns over again, in the opposite direction this time – another search on the library computers. Not for a name, but for a conference. The LTRR was the same as any other academic facility in that way; big noticeboards with old posters and old papers stuck to it. The intellectual bragging of its type. Some of the gatherings were small. Some, the interdisciplinary, were diverse and had larger attendances. People smiling over drinks, her predecessor with a glass in one hand and that same bit of silver glinting on her finger. The Bristlecone Pine studied the old programmes, the papers given and the photographs of conference dinners. They told her nothing.

It could have been anybody. It could have been nobody. She recognised a handful of her colleagues, scientists from other institutions that she'd met at other conferences, though those were few because she'd never had the standing or the funds to make regular appearances.

"I'd like to start changing that," she said, to the LTTR head at their next mixer. "I've been getting some fascinating results." She let herself talk, light and chatty, about archaeology and dwelling construction and it was all absolutely harmless. Unthreatening. Research that would make them look good in a number of ways, to a number of parties.

"I think that could be arranged," the head replied. "I'm glad to see you're settling in so well. Considering the circumstances."

"More challenging for the rest of you than for me," she replied. "Nothing to do with me really, I just kept my head down and got on with it. It must have been difficult for you all, though. I've been sorry for your loss," which was the most anodyne response she could think of, and designed to reinforce both her separation from the rest of them and her fundamental lack of interest.

Vacuity and disinterest had been her saving graces, and Bristlecone Pine reflected that if she had any sense she'd keep them on for more than just display. But they helped to send her to a conference, the largest one she'd ever been to – her paper, carefully written and absolutely irreproachable, was positively received – where she wandered through the crowds, with a friendly expression and a floating, flippant eye.

Could be anybody, could be nobody, she thought again, and she convinced herself it would be better to be nobody. Had almost succeeded, too, when she found herself face to face with another woman. One with a beautiful handbag, who smiled as much as Bristlecone Pine did. She also wore a ring. Small, not ostentatious, but recognisable for the cone picked out in silver on the top.

"I know that ring," said Bristlecone Pine, automatic, feeling denial in her mouth the minute she said it, half-wanting to take it back and not able to.

"It's a pretty thing, isn't it?" said the woman. "Common, too, I think. I picked it up at a market yesterday."

It sounded so perfect, but Bristlecone Pine knew deliberation when she heard it. Knew, too, the expression of a person taken up to mountains to see an ecosystem of margins, of high views and thin air. *Stupid,* she thought. *You're so stupid. It could mean throwing your whole career away. It could mean your life.*

"You didn't happen to lose a drive, did you?" she said. "Bright pink. I just found it."

"It could be one of mine," said the woman. She introduced herself. "I'm sorry," she said, peering at a conference badge that had twisted itself around. "You are?"

Are you a scientist, or aren't you?

"Unfortunately," said Bristlecone Pine, "I think I'm the replacement."

THE FISH-EATING SPIDER

For all the fish-eating spider is at home in water, it can die underground when forced there by predators. The Australian hunting wasp, Cryptocheilus australis, makes its burrows in clay or sand, out of reach of surf and fish. When the hunting wasp catches and stings a fish-eating spider, it drags the spider towards the burrow. The hunting wasp has been observed briefly abandoning the spider to return to its burrow and excavate it further, before returning to its prey. The fish-eating spider is dragged backwards by its pedipalps, and, paralysed, is stored in the burrow for eating.

#

The Fish-eating Spider preferred to do her work in Central Library. It was large and open and full of light, whereas the Science Library was dark and cramped and reminded her of burial and suffocation. It was exaggeration, she knew – she'd never been claustrophobic, but the sensation of weight never left. She was aware now, always, of the potential for danger.

It was something she'd never really considered, when she took on the job. Not seriously. The Stone Wētā had been clear, and the Fish-eating Spider couldn't honestly say that she hadn't been warned. But anger rising like the ocean and the opportunity to channel that anger into action was a temptation she couldn't resist. Given the choice again she'd make the same one – science had given her stability when everything else had been taken away, and to see that undermined as well . . . she didn't regret her decision.

The Fish-eating Spider just wished she could forget about it once in a while.

It made her wonder if that was the way of replacements. The Stone Wētā had gone to Mars, and it was an iconic trip, one which made the new colonists icons themselves. Larger than life, somehow, and the Fish-eating Spider felt herself small in comparison. Second-rate, without the skills or instincts of her predecessor.

The Stone Wētā wouldn't jump at every shadow, she thought, but it didn't stop her from jumping. And there was no-one she could go to for advice, not really. Another woman was on the ice, down in Antarctica studying creatures that weren't insects, so it wasn't as if the Fish-eating Spider could call her up and chat, even, without some excuse that would seem thin if looked at directly.

When communication could draw attention, sometimes it was better to be silent.

(Silence never helped anyone.)

The Fish-eating Spider gritted her teeth, chewed her nails to the quick and kept on regardless. She threw herself into research, that so-useful cover for operations and espionage, and was so productive that her supervisor was quickly impressed and then even more quickly worried.

"Burnout can be a genuine risk in grad students," said her supervisor. "Be careful you're not trying to do too much." There was a brief hesitation. "I've a responsibility to act in your best interests. You've been sick a lot recently. Run down. You look exhausted all the time. How are you sleeping?"

"Not so good," the Fish-eating Spider admitted. "But I've always been a night person."

"Nap in the day if you have to. Your work's been excellent, and you're well ahead of where you should be on your thesis right now. You can afford to slack off a bit. Go out with some mates, get some exercise. What about hobbies? You were excited about the university tramping club when you first came here. You still part of that?"

The Fish-eating Spider shrugged. "Sometimes." It was a hedge and they both knew it. She supposed that she should spend more time with the group, blend in better, but she wasn't sure she could stand the strain of socialising right then. She cast about for something else. "I used to swim a lot," she offered. "I miss it, but the ocean's so cold down here."

"There's the hot water salt pool out at St. Clair," said her supervisor. "You might want to think about giving it a go."

"I will," said the Fish-eating Spider. She said it as conciliation, mostly, knowing that the issue wouldn't drop. Even went out to the pool once, planning for it to be only the once – enough to show willing, to say that she'd gone, to placate her supervisor and not draw further attention to herself.

It had been a surprise, how wonderful it was. A poor replacement for the warmth of the waters further north, around the island she'd had to leave, but then she was a poor replacement herself. If she closed her eyes and floated, looked up at the sky – so clean and open – she could pretend an island familiarity enough for relaxation.

Always a water-baby. It was the way her mother described her, and the Fish-eating Spider was comforted by it, in the same way that the streams comforted her when she went out for fieldwork. She was a creature of surfaces and sky, no matter how many drives she covered over with deep earth. The more time she spent in the water, the easier it was to forget the nightmares of burial that kept her hunched and frozen, waiting for predators.

#

The fish-eating spider both swims and dives. It is able to do this because it is capable of breathing underwater. The spider is covered with short, thick hydrophobic hairs, and these hairs trap air bubbles so that they form a film over the legs and body of the spider. Lungs set beneath the abdomen open into this air-bubble film, allowing the spider to breathe – but these bubbles also increase its buoyancy, so the fish-eating spider has to catch hold of an underwater rock to prevent itself from rising to the surface.

#

With water as her touchstone, the Fish-eating Spider became

more proficient at navigating beneath surfaces. The sense of claustrophobia faded, and she was able to breathe more easily, restrict her sense of burial to data sets instead of self.

"Swimming's paying off then?" said her supervisor, appearing genuinely glad. The woman was also the head of department, and the Fish-eating Spider appreciated her consideration even as it made her wince with minor embarrassment at needing that consideration in the first place. "You've taken on a lot. I hate to think of you being overwhelmed."

"I'm good, thanks," said the Fish-eating Spider, which wasn't exactly true even if it was getting there, but she was able to put a better face on it at least, show a smooth surface. Her recovered water-sense helped: she pictured a thin sheen of liquid shielding her from the world, deceptively calm over depth.

She set data into caches, did her fieldwork, went swimming. She studied and rejoined the tramping club, made polite noises at the various Pacific Island organisations on campus. Tuvalu didn't have a club there – Tuvalu barely had islands anymore – and kind invitations to join in from her Cook Islands flatmate and the Fijian girl who worked across from her in the lab never quite panned out.

She missed her family. Spread out now across the Pacific, some in Australia, some in Auckland. One had gone to Canada, complaining all the time about the cold.

"I've started your brothers on lessons," said her mother, meaning language lessons. They'd picked up a little at home, Tuvaluan surviving in her parents' generation mostly, but many others in the community were fluent and the boys didn't want to stand out. The Fish-eating Spider remembered coming to New

Zealand, to higher land and away from drowning, remembered too how hard she'd worked to fit in, the struggle she'd had. How cut off she felt then. How cut off she felt now.

Science, for the Fish-eating Spider, represented a stability that made it easier to breathe. She caught it up and wrapped it round her, enjoyed the way it made the world make sense.

If it had been medicine, no-one would have minded so much. "She could have been a doctor," her mother said. "But no! It's always spiders . . ."

Her mother was not fond of spiders. She tried to show an interest, but the Fish-eating Spider could always see her glazing over or, worse, biting her tongue. A doctor could have bought a lot of language lessons, a lot of sports equipment. And it was science, too, and the Fish-eating Spider could have gone to the zoo on her weekends if she liked animals so much.

"I want something to put my back against," the Fish-eating Spider had argued. "Something solid."

"And helping other people isn't solid enough for you?"

"The science I do helps too," said the Fish-eating Spider, knowing as she did that for her mother it was an unconvincing argument. Partly because there wasn't much practical use in knowing about spiders, not in this country at least – it'd be different in Australia – and partly because, since Tuvalu, her mother had lost faith in the ability of scientists to do much of anything anyway, unless they had a stethoscope and the wherewithal to pay the mortgage.

"Look how much good science did for us," she finished, always, and there was nothing that the Fish-eating Spider could say to that because it was true. The science was clear and present and ignored, and the rising waters had taken what an entire nation had never wanted to give. "If it could have helped then why didn't it?"

Explanations of other interests induced nothing but tears and arguments. It was an old argument anyway, and old acceptance – that money and power had tipped the balance instead of reason, that the earth and the sea were tools for exploitation only, and the little people of the world could do nothing about it but come to understand abandonment.

It had been that more than anything else that had induced the Fish-eating Spider to take up the Stone Wētā on her offer, joining a resistance that seemed a thin and filmy thing itself to hang a method on. To join the Stone Wētā, who was abandoning in her own way, leaving a planet instead of an island and leaving it voluntarily, leaving the rest of them to clean up the mess. Forced migration was a different thing entirely, and for all the Fish-eating Spider had tried to assimilate she had been a person, once, who had a home and now that home was gone.

She wasn't about to let another home be taken from her, and the destabilisation of science, the mutilation of it by the same forces that had taken an island, was a threat to stability and belonging. To keep that, the Fish-eating Spider would learn to breathe beneath the surface. She'd learn to conceal and adapt, to breathe her burials.

She'd do it because, unlike Tuvalu, that information one day would be able to come back. The Fish-eating Spider simply wouldn't tolerate any less.

#

The fish-eating spider relies on ambush rather than on tunnel or webs. It waits on the edge of pools or streams and by resting its legs on the surface of the water, as if it were silk, is able to detect the ripples that signify prey. After the detection of this prey, the fish-eating spider runs along the surface of the water to trap the fish with its front legs. Once the animal is securely caught it is paralysed by an injection of neurotoxin, and its flesh is liquefied by the digestive enzymes of the fish-eating spider, which tows it through the water and back to shore for feeding.

#

Field work always increased in the summer. The Fish-eating Spider went out looking for egg sacs, peered closely beside rivers, enjoyed her bush walking. She had a number of field sites, and some of them were remote, but there were enough small landmarks that a periodic visitor could find more than arachnids, and leave more than footprints.

Most of the time she went alone. Occasionally members of the tramping club went with her, or other of the grad students – doing field work alone could be frowned on, but the Fish-eating Spider was responsible in the bush, an experienced tramper, and so her trips were winked at. She'd always preferred tramping alone anyway, but refusing company might have been noticed, and so she took her mates from the club when they asked, recruited them into spider hunting with rewards of chocolate and made no indication of caches. That meant she had to keep certain drives for longer than she would have liked, sometimes, but it was better than risking the alternative if someone woke up in the night to the sound of digging, and a spade hitting metal.

At first the Fish-eating Spider was all nerves and frustration, the desire to bury and be done, but as the water and the normalisation of her new life proceeded apace she began to relax into guardianship. Not that she ever became sloppy – the drives stayed on her at all times, except in the swimming pool when they were hidden in a small waterproof compartment in her bag, and she always had half a dozen of her own small data devices for it to blend in with, the same as any student did. But for all that the water calmed her and took her thoughts from burial, the Fish-eating Spider began to wonder if it was also enhancing her instincts, for along the back of her spine she began to feel a distant sensation of movement. It made her scared, again, but it also made her quietly, burningly angry.

There was nothing to make her suspicions concrete, not at first, but when one of her lab mates slammed the door of the computer room the department's grad students all shared, complaining of theft, the Fish-eating Spider felt the vibrations of the slam in the tips of her fingers.

There'd been a spate of break-ins in the student flats. Televisions taken, mostly, and computers. The odd stereo, hoarded bottles of spirits. "It's my own fault," said her lab mate. "It's not like we weren't warned to be careful locking up," with the university sending out emails full of security advice. "Whoever it was went through my jewellery box, the bastards. And my knicker drawer!"

"That's just disgusting," said the Fish-eating Spider. "Creeps."

Probably a perfectly normal burglar, but after that, every day for a month, the Fish-eating Spider left her drives out in full view in the shared room, next to her laptop and her notes. She wasn't holding anything for burial so left them all as bait, set up a tiny camera hidden by a bookshelf – all the old back issues of *Nature* and *Science*, the *New Zealand Journal of Marine and Freshwater Research*, that no-one ever looked at anyway when e-copies were available.

She always locked the door. It might look premeditated otherwise. And when one day she saw the drives taken and copied, put back carefully into their original position and the door locked again behind, she didn't report it.

On the bright side, it wasn't anyone that she knew. The Fish-eating Spider had distant doubts, borne of the Stone Wētā, that anyone dodgy could have gotten past the department head, but every time she met with the woman for supervision she couldn't bring herself to comment in case those doubts lacked merit. Instead, she kept herself alert and watchful, waiting for tremors. There was nothing incriminating in those copied drives, nothing in her lab mate's drawers either. It had the feel of a fishing expedition. The Fish-eating Spider was competent enough at those, sharing a skill-set with her thesis subject and frequently taking fishing gear out to the rivers when she researched.

But fishing expedition or not, the Fish-eating Spider did not like to be hunted. Seasons of prowling the riverbanks of the South Island for prey had made her far more comfortable with hunting. So she said nothing, did nothing, just fumed beneath the surface and waited.

Only afterwards, pulling into the lonely exit by a distant track, did she allow herself to acknowledge that anger had clouded her judgement. She'd posted on social media, as she usually did before a trip, listing the plants and animals she hoped to see – the tramping club had a bingo sheet going, and the member who photographed them all first would win a new pair of boots. "Going hunting for spiders – and tree wētā!" she posted, wearing her tramping club shirt and a big grin.

The tree wētā was on the bingo sheet, but for all its rocky name, the stone wētā was of the genus *Hemideina* – commonly known as the tree wētā genus.

The Fish-eating Spider set up camp by her field site stream and waited. When she saw the same face on the track as she did on the camera, felt the vibrations of his steps, she hit him hard from behind with a tree branch.

#

The fish-eating spider is the only New Zealand spider to have been observed catching fish. It is a nocturnal hunter. (Others of the same genus also hunt on or near water, but are more restricted in their diets, catching primarily insects – which the fish-eating spider Dolomedes dondalei also eats, dragging insects such as crane flies below the surface of the water.) It is theorised that fish-eating spiders – albeit of different species – are more likely to exist in warmer waters, as less oxygen in those waters forces fish to swim closer to the water's surface.

#

"I don't know who the hell you are," said the Fish-eating Spider, grim as she finished tying fishing line around his arms and ankles, "but don't think I don't know you've been following me. Who are you? What do you want?"

"You've made a mistake," said the man. There was a small trickle of blood oozing down his cheek but all the Fish-eating Spider knew about head wounds was they bled a lot. That *wasn't* a lot, so she was prepared to believe it only a tiny graze. He seemed to be over the worst of the stunning, at any rate.

"I don't think so." The Fish-eating Spider would have liked to believe that he was telling the truth, that there was an innocent explanation or that he was just a garden variety pervert, someone who got off creeping on girls, searching their drawers and their drives for sex tapes. Any such hope had died as he woke up tied in fishing line – there'd been an initial struggle against the line, very brief, and then he'd stilled entirely, calm and alert.

If anyone had trussed up the Fish-eating Spider with fishing line she'd have screamed her head off.

"You're not afraid. There's something . . . wrong about that."

"I'm afraid."

"You hide it very well. And you haven't answered my question. Who are you? Why are you following me?"

"I'm not following you."

"Liar."

"Look, you obviously don't want to believe me. So why don't you just call the cops and they can sort it out. If I'm as dodgy as you think they'll take care of it."

"I'm not calling the police," said the Fish-eating Spider, and the man laughed at her.

"So you're going to untie me, let me walk out of here? You can't think I'm that dangerous, then. Might as well do it now.

123

Whatever you might think, I don't want to hurt you. You're just a kid."

The Fish-eating Spider didn't bother to reply. A small part of her wondered if it might unnerve him, but mostly she was just too angry to speak. Tired and scared and *angry*, and she settled herself down with her back to a tree, the river by her side, and let her hand trail in the water, let the chill of it cool her as well, and stared at him.

"Going to be like that then, is it?" he said. "You going to try and wait me out? Let me sit here until I piss myself, maybe I'll get angry too, say things I don't mean to until you hear what you want?" He shifted a little, and the Fish-eating Spider watched, dispassionate. She'd tied those knots well and good. He wasn't getting out of them in a hurry and it couldn't be comfortable being trussed up like that.

She couldn't bring herself to feel sorry.

"I'm not your enemy," he said. "Look, cards on the table. I'm not a spider kind of guy. I was looking for wētā, instead I got you. You're mixed up in something that maybe you shouldn't be. You know it and I know it and you know that I know it. But it's something that can be worked out, and to both our benefits.

"I really have no interest in hurting you," he repeated. "I've a daughter your age. It'd just be wrong. And I know how I'd feel if someone took advantage of her, got her into trouble because she was young and idealistic and wanted to do good. But you've got to understand there are lots of ways of doing good. And yeah, there are some things we can't change that maybe we could have done differently in the past, but when the chance for change is over, all you can do is position yourself to take advantage of the world that's coming. That's what I'd tell my little girl if she were in your position."

"I'm not your little girl," said the Fish-eating Spider, and the man nodded.

"No. My girl's got her whole life set up. No student loan, no debt. When she's finished school there's a good job waiting for her, a down payment for a house. All because her dad's a businessman, who's made it his business to understand how economics works. Wouldn't you like that? Security, a place to go?"

The Fish-eating Spider turned her head, tried not to listen. She watched her fingers comb through the surface of the water, tried not to think of her student loan, the family disappointment when she'd gone into ecology instead of medicine. There was so much that needed helping out with, her younger brothers, her parents getting on now and still scraping to pay the mortgage.

She knew what was being dangled in front of her, water being made to ripple to see if she would pounce. The hell of it was she was actually tempted. Spiders didn't pay the bills.

Spiders were never so angry. The Fish-eating Spider felt the anger boil in her – anger at him, at the Stone Wētā for getting her involved in the first place. Anger at herself for choosing to get involved, for being weak and tempted anyway. A tear welled up, rolled down her cheek. It felt as hot as lava, as hot as toxin.

"Jesus. Don't cry. She should be shot, getting a kid like you caught up in this. It'll ruin your life. There's no need. I can give you a much better option – there are people out there who'll pay for loyalty like yours, and pay well. Try to think of a better life than this. Don't you want that?"

A life away from riverbanks, from the scent of the bush at night, a life of hurt and hunting, of hiding . . .

"Come on," he said. "Untie me, why don't you. Let me take you home."

"I can't go home," said the Fish-eating Spider, forlorn. "Home's gone. It drowned. The water came and took it. Because of people like you," she said, the crouching instinct rising up in an angry burn now, the stream through her fingers a reminder and an end to restraint. "You and your money and power and *business*, as though that was the important thing. The only important thing. And my home is gone and drowned and there's nothing to go back to. Don't you understand?" she said, her voice rising into wail. "It *drowned*."

The fishing line was slippery, and he fought as she dragged him to the stream, but in the end the home of the Fish-eating Spider was not the only thing to be forced under the surface and kept there.

THE GYMPIE GYMPIE

The gympie gympie leaf retains less water and toughens with age. While all of the gympie gympie's leaves are nutritious the youngest are the most so, and they are produced throughout the year. This makes the gympie gympie vulnerable to herbivorous grazing. The stinging hairs that cover the leaves are however densest in the younger leaves, which may discourage some herbivores. Each hair is so extremely fine that the skin frequently closes over them, making them difficult to see and extract.

#

The Gympie Gympie had never thought herself a mentor, but a directive had come out of Mali and she'd found herself at a Pacific-based conference of indigenous women in science, and there was a girl curled in on herself and shivering.

"I didn't know what to do," she said, after the Gympie Gympie rousted her out of her cheap hotel room and took her for a walk in a park that had lots of space in it and very few people. "I couldn't drag him all the way back to the car. So I just dug a really, really big hole a couple of hundred metres off the track and left him there."

"Did you get rid of the fishing line?"

The girl looked sick. "Yes. It . . . it left *marks* all on the skin though. You know, ligatures. I wouldn't have been able to take him back to his car if I wanted to. Even if I crashed it, anyone who saw the . . . the body would have known."

"What did you do with his car?"

"Dumped it in a river. There were recent rains, it was all swollen."

The Gympie Gympie had seen the news articles – a tourist missing, presumed drowned after his vehicle went off the road. A search party swept the river for several days, but the body was never recovered.

"Any chance anyone saw you do it?"

The Fish-eating Spider shook her head. "It was in the middle of the night. The middle of the bush. Took me a day and a half to walk back to my car."

She'd had the sense to cover her tracks at least, though how long that would last the Gympie Gympie didn't know. Depended on how much suspicion was raised – though for some, the suspicion itself would be confirmation.

"Sounds like you did the right thing to me," she said, and the Fish-eating Spider just gaped at her, frozen into place as if all her legs had been cut off.

"I *killed* a man," she said, verging on tears and hysteria.

"The way you tell it, it was probably quick," said the Gympie Gympie. "Could have been a lot worse." In her own country at least, spider bites could mean pain and vomiting, muscular weakness, and that didn't even touch what the plants might do to you. She shrugged. "If you want to call it worse."

It gave her some satisfaction to see the girl flinch back as if slapped, her sudden burst into uncontrollable weeping. The Gympie Gympie directed her to the base of a nearby tree, one isolated enough that she could see anyone coming, and sat down with her, let the girl cry herself out. In her experience, covering over injury, leaving the problem buried before healing, produced nothing but ulcers.

"Feel better?" she said afterwards, offering tissues. "No? Well, you probably won't for a while, and that's alright. It shouldn't be an easy thing, killing. It shouldn't be anything you ever like to do – but it's alright to do it if it saves your life."

"What if it didn't save my life?" said the Fish-eating Spider, red-rimmed about the eyes and clutching her tissues. "He said he wasn't going to hurt me. He said he wanted to help."

"You think he was telling the truth?'

There was a long silence. The Gympie Gympie hoped that silence came from close consideration, but one look at the girl's face indicated exhausted confusion more than anything else. "I think about that all the time," she said. "All the time since it happened. I don't know. I just don't know. He might have been lying . . . but what if he wasn't? How do I know?"

"You might not ever," said the Gympie Gympie. "That's something you're going to have to learn to live with. And take it from someone who's been there: you *can* live with it."

#

The gympie gympie – like the bristlecone pine – is a species reliant upon colonisation. It does well in bright light, such as that caused by disturbances in forest environments. This makes it a particularly difficult consequence of human disturbance. Deforestation, logging, and even the establishment of walking tracks frequently encourages rapid gympie gympie growth.

#

When the Gympie Gympie built defences over her own information caches, she did so with the full knowledge that ecology would help it along. The full knowledge, too, that such a defence might be needed.

A resistance built out of disturbance and colonisation was one she'd been prepared for her whole life. That preparation had the histories of nations and peoples behind it, and the Gympie Gympie knew from her ancestors what happened to a community when it was colonised by those with an ideology that excused killing. There were enough dead relatives in her family tree who'd had that particular experience, and so it wasn't hard for her to recognise a conflict in the coming.

There was bitterness in the recognition: for all the undermining of science, the destruction of the environment thereby – even the destruction in turn of scientists who stood up to it – there was no-one looking at the last and justifying it through inhumanity. Money, yes. Power too, and these things had always been at the root of colonisation. It's just that now no-one bothered to hide it.

Lobbyists in Canberra, in capitals all over, arguing that

restrictions were uneconomic, that good business meant bad sacrifice. They could afford to buy votes, the oil companies and the miners, the ones who didn't care if the Reef went or the ecosystem died around them. They did it in daylight, too, because colonisation was always a bright and progressive perception, moving forward into Terra Nullius, opening up the empty lands for opportunity and profit.

Having lived the other side of that equation, the Gympie Gympie thought disturbance should be used to benefit, for once, in more ways than the trickle-down that had never actually trickled down to any community she'd ever felt at home in.

Using their own tactics against them gave bitter satisfaction. The logging roads, the fragment forests. If she picked a random spot and walked there, even, her body breaking through undergrowth would let little patches of extra light reach down to the soil of her footsteps and encourage growth there.

The act of burial was protection twice over. It was also, though she rarely admitted it, an act of invitation.

Removing the plant caused its own problems. Even without the stinging hairs, cutting or slashing could cause allergic reactions, and the Gympie Gympie had often observed forestry workings wearing gloves and respirators while trying to remove her namesake.

Then again, they were used to dealing with it. Most people were unfamiliar, and the Gympie Gympie didn't know if anyone had followed her into the bush looking for retrieval, or even confirmation, but she hoped they had. She had hundreds of caches scattered through the bush, held a map of them in her mind only and knew how many of them were fake. Perhaps a dozen or so actually held smuggled data. The rest of them were blinds, and the Gympie Gympie hoped that they would.

She remembered all too well the stories she'd read as a child, as an adult. Someone who'd been stung and had to be strapped, screaming, to his bed. Another person who'd shot himself to end the pain. Horses driven mad from it, running over cliffs. Research for chemical weapons.

(Stolen generations. White Australia, land appropriated, land degraded. Infectious diseases, massacres, genocide.)

Land lost to farming that never recovered – an ecology ill-adapted to sheep and cattle. Soil salinity, dryland salinity, and the changing climate making none of it better. People seemed to want to learn the hard way. The Gympie Gympie had learned the hard way at her grandmother's knee, a history of hardship. She learned it again in her schooling, the difference between expectation and exploitation, the time it took for ecosystem to recover, the need for ecosystem recovery for the people who were part of it.

Learned, too, how little learning counted for anything. How easily it could be brushed aside as if learning were for little people, and knowing better a thing that could be bought, and the little people along with it.

The Gympie Gympie was not little, and she could not be bought. She was sunlight and adaptation; she was responsibility and response mechanism. She had a number of ways to protect herself and chose to use so few of them because her perceived vulnerability, in full light, attracted predators.

#

These painful hairs – which cover the gympie gympie's stem and fruits as well as its leaves – can also be dislodged by the wind and either breathed in, or shed on the ground around the gympie gympie, essentially contaminating the area and potentially causing allergic reactions in grazing mammals.

#

"It's not wrong to protect yourself," said the Gympie Gympie to the Fish-eating Spider. "Or to protect what you care about. Sometimes that means extreme measures."

"You're really advocating murder?"

"I'm advocating self-defence, actually," said the Gympie Gympie. She recalled a scientist who'd worked with gympie gympie and developed such a severe allergy to those hairs that she was advised to quit working with them after face masks and welding gloves while handling the plant didn't keep her out of hospital. "Where are you from again? Planning on a return trip anytime soon? No? I'm not sitting and waiting until my homelands are as unrecoverable as yours."

"And you're prepared to kill for that." It wasn't a question.

"I'm prepared to let other people kill themselves for it at the very least," the Gympie Gympie replied. "It's not my fault if ignorance gives them a screaming death. Maybe they'll get lucky, try to scrub the hairs out in a river and a croc will take them."

"How's that lucky?" blurted the Fish-Eating Spider.

The Gympie Gympie shrugged. "It's quick," she said. "Look, don't ask me for sympathy. These people have none for us. And we hide and scheme and bury and that's great, I'm not doubting the validity of what we do – it's a necessary thing. But it's not enough. As far as I'm concerned justice can be bought. It has been. All these corporations and politicians, they've got money behind them, they've all got lawyers to protect them. What do we have? We've got what we know. I say use it. They want to come onto my land, they want to hunt me down on my land? I know it better than they do."

Her own namesake, salting the ground with the tiny silica shreds of its body – waiting to be inhaled, to be ground in. "All you need to do is stand near it to get sick," she said. "Maybe if a few more scientists reacted that way there wouldn't be so much rush to discredit them."

It was an ongoing argument. The Sand Cat, deep in the Mali desert, had an admiration for pacifism that the Gympie Gympie did not always share. "I've seen what bullets do," the other woman had said, but she'd also acknowledged that she wasn't a leader in more than data, and that she had no legitimacy, or even the desire, to try and force a wider obedience.

"Resistance is survival," said the Gympie Gympie. "And survival's a way of fighting back – but it's not the only way."

"I'd hoped for more than survival," said the Fish-eating Spider. "When I agreed . . . when I agreed to help, to come in and help hide, it was because I was angry. It seemed all the people around me were gutless. I think I almost wanted the danger. I certainly wanted to fight."

"Well, you got your chance," said the Gympie Gympie.

"And I keep wondering if it was necessary."

"Hindsight," said the Gympie Gympie. "What do you think would have happened, had you let him go? You really think it would have been over, that it would have been easy? That you'd say no thank you, and he'd say hey, I had to try and you'd both go your own ways? I know you're new at this, but you're not that ignorant. Whoever brought you in would have told you what's happened to some of us."

"He said he had a daughter my age."

"Maybe he did. I know someone else who had a kid, and she disappeared on the way back from her field site. Probably dead in a ditch right now. You think that's what she heard – we both want a better world for our kids, can't we talk about this? Won't you at least listen to what we have to offer?"

It was plausible enough. The Gympie Gympie had never met the woman, but buried under a stinging shrub, just off a smooth-barked kauri she'd known since she was six, was a drive of her research, the parts of it she couldn't get published. She'd lain awake at night after, wondering about the old silence from the southwest, the new silence out of Madagascar. The rumours of someone taken off the ice.

"Tell me something," she said. "This man you couldn't have carried back to the car." The man she'd drowned, the man she dragged through undergrowth and buried deeper than data. "Could he have carried you?"

The Fish-eating Spider was tall, her arms and back heavy with corded muscle. She had the look of a swimmer, the Gympie Gympie thought, and not someone who could be easily hefted. "I'm just saying," she said. "You're a student. It's probably been drummed into you to leave plans behind when you're out on field trips."

"And when I'm tramping," said the Fish-eating Spider,

automatic in her addition. The bush didn't suffer fools, and isolation mixed with ignorance was a recipe for hurt.

"He couldn't have left you there. You'd have been found straight off."

"He could have just buried me," said the Fish-eating Spider. "Like I did to him."

"You'd have to give up information very quickly yourself for that to be an option," said the Gympie Gympie.

#

The gympie gympie is an inveterate grudge holder. Not only does the pain from its sting last – potentially for years after an animal has been stung – but even a herbarium sample that has been stored for decades in a museum is able to sting.

#

She'd realised early on that data was a weapon. That the suppression of data was being used against scientists, and against any possible amelioration of climate. Realised, too, that in preserving data she was weaponising it as well. The Gympie Gympie wasn't holding information for the Sand Cat, not really. She was holding arms.

The lack of surprise was what had surprised her. She'd been out in the bush one day, the trees overhead, the liana draped over them and the nettles far enough away, and there'd been a dull burst in her heart that was all acknowledgement. How quickly she'd recognised the necessity, how she'd never been any less than certain. What *was* surprising was how long it had taken her to realise that information was not the only weapon needed.

It was a loose organisation, the Sand Cat's. Cleverly administered, she did admit – the small cells given autonomy, mostly, and kept apart so that any breach would only be minimally damaging. An organisation, too, where collaboration was a driving force, and where respect for reasoned dissent was paramount. A necessary factor for scientists, many of whom had volunteered to protect data in the first place because they felt the stifling of method in its suppression. For people who were accustomed to testing and scepticism, it was an undermining too far. Made them feel not-scientists, corrupt in themselves and in their work. That fundamental allegiance to dissent didn't go away when the question of loyalties became political. Each one of them had a background that underpinned their views, and if that background was shared when it came to the universality of the scientific method, it was the personal history and culture through which they viewed that method that spoke to them of the conflict to come.

"Power has no moral compass," said the Gympie Gympie. "It has no pity, and its memory is long. Mine is longer."

The memory of a people going back for so many millennia. "We thought isolation could keep us safe," she said. "We couldn't fathom what another people might do to us. And look what happened.

"I will not make that mistake again," she said.

"It's not a mistake to hold back from violence when you can," said the Sand Cat.

"Of course not. But it is a mistake not to realise when violence is coming that sometimes that's all you can meet it with. We are at war," said the Gympie Gympie. "It is a war that has sunk islands and made deserts where trees have been. It is a war that may include the starvation of millions. There's going to come a point," she said, "when saving data is not enough."

She knew not all the women agreed with her. Most of them didn't know, most likely, that she even existed – she herself knew only half a dozen or so for certain. Had never tried to know more, aware of the danger that could come after capture. But the Gympie Gympie, with the history of one slaughtered people behind her, believed that there were other operatives with a similar history. And all of them, she thought, were more than usually sceptical of the self-made limitations of power.

Theirs was a passive resistance. There was value in that, and the Gympie Gympie was proud of the work that she'd done. She just believed, deep in the bones of her, that it wouldn't be enough.

"And part of you thinks the same," she said. "Your people kept their knowledge close, hid it in houses and smuggled it out and kept it from bonfires. But the people who would have lit the match of those fires didn't leave your city peacefully."

Timbuktu had needed soldiers for that.

All of the women, all of the scientists. Crouching down and surviving, keeping data safe in deserts and in rainforests, in polar ice and outer space and inner planets, in coastal waters and mountain mesas. Who would their soldiers be?

#

Despite the dangerous nature of the plants, some animals have developed strategies for navigating their presence. The plant is eaten by a number of insects and other small animals, and birds disperse the gympie gympie's fruit. It is theorised, however, that the venom from the gympie gympie evolved as a response to a significant predator that no longer exists. With little cause to keep such a monstrous response to grazing, observation of some individual gympie gympie trees indicates that they are becoming an almost painless experience. The silica stings remain, but the venom is either altered or absent.

#

The Gympie Gympie shuffled a little against the tree, shifted her position slightly so that she was full in the afternoon's fading sunlight.

"I don't know if I can be like you," said the Fish-eating Spider. Her tears were long gone, but her eyes still red and puffy. She'd have to lie down with a cold flannel over them if she wanted to turn up for the morning session without drawing too much attention.

"You don't have to be. It takes all sorts. For me, it helps to think of every day as a battle. Maybe one day I'll begin to feel differently. Start planting something else. Something a little less poisonous. It's a nice dream, anyway."

"You don't think it's going to happen."

The Gympie Gympie shook her head. "There's a tipping point coming," she said. "Too many disappearing now, and on both sides. Eventually we're not going to be able to pretend anymore, and it'll all come out. Them, us. I guess we'll find out how much power's really changed over the past few hundred years, eh? We'll find out how much of it is ours, now."

"They know it's me, don't they?" said the Fish-eating Spider. She looked very young. "The people who sent him. They know it's me. They know what I did."

"Very probably yes," said the Gympie Gympie. "They could probably prove it too. Find the body, provide the forensics. But there'd be questions they'd have to answer. Potential exposure. Bribes and lobbyists are one thing, murder's another. We could argue in a fair court, if such a thing exists anymore, that it was self-defence on your part. Enough to muddy the waters. More likely he'll stay missing."

"You can't send me any more drives," said the Fish-eating Spider. "I'd hide them for you, I would, but they might be able to get the person sending them to me. You can't risk it."

"I know. Don't worry, it's taken care of." The Sand Cat had set up a network of layers and layers, like the grains of sand dunes. Blow on it, and all the grains scattered – or all the hairs came out, which was a metaphor more to the Gympie Gympie's taste.

"But . . . I don't understand. If you'd already thought of that, if there aren't going to be any more drives sent my way, then why are you even talking to me? Why is whoever it is, wherever she is, even bothering?"

The Gympie Gympie tilted her head and stared. "Why wouldn't she bother?" she said. "Why wouldn't I? Did you think you'd just be ditched?"

"I'm not useful anymore. You said so yourself."

"That doesn't mean you don't matter," said the Gympie

Gympie, scoffing. "You stood up when many wouldn't have. You helped. And you got hurt because of it."

"I think you mean I did the hurting," said the Fish-eating Spider.

"No, I didn't," said the Gympie Gympie, and her tone was definite. "You're not disposable." Not one of the little people, to be run over for the convenience and profit of others. "What kind of resistance d'you think we're running here anyway? We're all responsible for each other. I could help you so I did. Simple as that."

"It's *not* that simple, actually," said the Fish-eating Spider, and there was a stubborn set of her jaw that the Gympie Gympie liked better than tears. "How did you even know I exist? How did you know what I did?"

"She told me. The woman who runs this thing," said the Gympie Gympie. "We don't agree on a lot of things. Opposite ends of the scale, you'd say. We've got very different ideas about what it means to fight, and what's coming, and what's necessary. She knows our differences as well as I do. That's why she sent me to you – to this bloody conference. She thought I'd be able to help you better than anyone else."

The Fish-eating Spider wasn't done. "Doesn't my being here put you in danger?"

"Maybe," said the Gympie Gympie, and she was almost indifferent. "I prepared for that too." She hoped she was followed home, she really did.

Wondered, too, if she'd been sent to encourage such a following. She didn't believe that the Sand Cat was at the point where the realities of escalating conflict were more powerful than optimism, but she couldn't be sure. Perhaps this was a dual opportunity for her, this trip. Triple, even, because she had data to pass on, and the same to take away again for storage. But that someone else could have done in her place, if necessary. She didn't know anyone else who was equipped to deal with the Fish-eating Spider, though.

Perhaps she really had been sent only to help. Admittedly, she didn't know how much help she'd been able to provide. Sympathy, mostly, the chance to confess. A little absolution – though only a little, because the Gympie Gympie didn't believe much wrong had been done, and allowing the girl to wallow helped no-one. What was done was done, and there were bigger battles ahead.

She looked forward to the day they were done.

She looked forward to the day that they started.

THE FISH-SCALE GECKO

The fish-scale gecko is able to shed its skin and remain unharmed because its skin – which has larger scales than any other gecko – has adapted to this particular defence mechanism. The narrow point of scale attachment is relatively small compared to the surface area of the scale, requiring less force to remove. Furthermore, the skin beneath the scale has a pre-formed splitting zone so that detachment occurs relatively easily and without bleeding.

#

For the Fish-scale Gecko, the resumption of normal life was a simpler thing than she expected. She'd lived that simple life – complicated only by the mundane concerns of everyone around her: keeping family, making rent – for years, and its resurrection was like waking from the dream of another world.

She did her best not to think of it. She told herself that this was because it was easier to behave normally if she thought normally, and not in terms of secrecy and resistance, and this wasn't a newly formed strategy but rather one she'd learned to rely on during her time as an active operant. So much of her recent life had been spent watching, and waiting . . . for data to come to her, for an opportunity to stash that data, and for her involvement to be discovered. The weight of it had started to affect the way she walked, shoulders hunched all the way in, a constant tension headache. It had been an effort every day to act as if she were normal, and all her activities above any possible reproach. Feeling as if she were being watched every second, knowing that beneath the paranoia was an element of truth.

Less action didn't mean less thought, and if she loosed her hold on the latter she'd be hunching again for news kept away from her, from the reports of other countries and other scientists. Anyone watching would see no change in her behaviour – she still made scouting trips into the forest, into the karst, and if on these she wasn't closing in on a cache she was looking at new sites for tourism, trying to merge economics with conservation in a way would keep ecology alive, and the local people with it.

The Fish-scale Gecko told herself she kept thoughtless for consistency, but it was not the only reason.

She was jealous.

Of all the stupid things, she thought, walking under hot sun and with the warmth of the forest rising high around her. *As if there's anything for you to be jealous of.* Fear, frustration. The potential for peril, for disappearance and no-one knew what ending. But there'd been excitement in it too, and adrenaline she only felt in tree-tops, looking down at the world below. Seeing how far she could fall, how easily it could all be taken from her.

There was vindication, as well. Pride. Even a self-satisfaction of sorts, that she had her ethics and a readiness to stand up for them, that she'd come to the true testing time of her vocation and hadn't failed, hadn't turned away from her own principles.

It would have been so easy to be bought. It would have been easier, even, to look away and do nothing – but she hadn't, and she'd been part of a group who hadn't, and she *missed* it, the camaraderie and the sharing of danger, the shared sense of purpose.

She wanted it back so badly. Could hardly keep from reaching out, even knowing the danger of it, to insert herself back into a movement that other people still got to be a part of.

The only reason she didn't risk herself that way was the knowledge that she'd risk others as well, so she chose not to think on it, not to remember, lest the acid swell of jealousy in her stomach overwhelm good sense, undermine what she'd work so hard for, jeopardise her clean escape.

There was, after all, other work that she could do.

"It's hard moving from what you know," she said, on her trips to the villages, on her meetings with people who kept themselves alive through work on the margins, illegal forestry or slogging in sapphire mines. "It's hard to stand up for something new. To learn to do things a new way, when you can still get by with the old." But eco-tourism was a hope that they could have a way to keep the forest alive and their families with it, and if the Fish-scale Gecko could learn subterfuge for necessity then they could learn sustainability for it as well.

"I'll help you," she said. "This is our home here, our heritage. We can save it together if we want to."

#

The fish-scale gecko can remove more than just its skin. Like the other members of its genus, the gecko is also able to shed its tail in order to escape from predators. The fish-scale gecko can replace both skin and tail relatively easily, and so successfully that each replacement is barely noticeable. Shedding its skin leaves the fish-scale gecko with no scars, and it is frequently only possible to determine if a tail is original or a later addition by X-raying the gecko to check for missing vertebrae.

#

Conservation had become a weighted word. A political word, and a personal one, until all the meanings of it blurred together. So much of what it represented was linked to absence, and the Fish-scale Gecko, as she waited and pretended, was able to add another link to that association. Ironic, that she could best support conservation now by her absence. The Sand Cat had built a network and the kernel of it had been African women, until they were able to branch out, become more global in their outlook. With her removal from active work, the Fish-scale Gecko had lost that community of women like herself. Contact between them now would only endanger and, bereft, she was left to mourn a community she might never be part of again.

"There's got to be a contingency," said the Sand Cat, in the first days after the first woman disappeared, and the data left dumb behind her. "If one of us is found out."

"We can't just wait to be picked off, one by one," argued the Japanese Sea Star. "We need a way to hide women as well as information."

A necessary conversation, but one which had made the Fish-scale Gecko shudder. She was a creature of heights and canopy. Most of the data she'd heard of, the rumours of other women and the hiding places they chose, was a lot closer to *underneath*, and she didn't enjoy her claustrophobia.

"How can we even know," she said. "We're not spies, not really. None of us! It's guesswork and instinct and we're trying." Doing well even, for women faced with work they weren't trained for, gritting teeth and getting on. "And if someone panics and runs off before they should, if they think they've been recognised and haven't, all they're going to do is draw attention. It's better to stay put," she said. "Our advantage is that we know our own communities. We've all got neighbours, colleagues." People who knew them, who would come to help if they heard screaming, who might recognise a wrongness.

That had been the Sand Cat's recommendation right from the start. "I don't need the reminder," she said.

"I think you do," said the Fish-scale Gecko. But she said it kindly, because that first disappearance meant they had blood on their hands, all of them. Every woman involved, who had chosen to be involved, who had come in believing that they knew the risks. "And I'm the one who's asked them to do it," said the Sand Cat. "Even when it's not me personally, it's someone who can be traced back to me."

"I'm not doing this for you," said the Fish-scale Gecko. "This isn't a cult of personality. I got involved to protect the science. I'd like to think I'd be doing that whether I knew you or not."

And that was the truth – but it was also true that it was easier to be brave as part of a group. And all of them, everywhere, were just a few small strands away from being cut off from that group, from a compromise that had to see data moved elsewhere. "It's knowing whether or not you've been compromised that's the problem," she continued. "It'd be easy if we knew for sure. But if we don't know . . . if we're left alone, all of us, someone's likely to panic."

They'd do it with the best of intentions. Sacrifice themselves, even, to lead the threat away, but intent didn't mitigate outcome and that sacrifice, made before time, could be a long and costly one.

"I will not tell women they have to stay and even die if they are afraid, or if they are found," said the Sand Cat. "I will not do it."

"I don't think you understand," said the Fish-scale Gecko. "No-one ever said that you had to ask. We knew what we were getting into, all of us." It was presumption to speak for them all, she knew, but no-one could bury data – literally bury it – without thinking of the need, and of what the acknowledgement of that need implied. "You have tapped into a population that tends to understand equations," she said. "One life against the climate?"

They all had homes. They all had places that they loved.

"It's not your place to make that decision for us," she said. She might have to run, one day. She might not. She might have to leave everything behind, shed her old life and start again in a harsher world, but advice or not, friendship or not – conspiracy or not – that decision was hers to make.

Its physiological escape mechanisms mean that the fish-scale gecko is very difficult to catch. Even a loose grip causes it to shed its skin and run for cover, and captured specimens are often damaged in this way, making investigation of entirely intact geckos a rarity. Even capturing them with wads of cotton is insufficient to prevent damage.

#

Jealousy. Indecision. The awareness of threat, both to herself and to science. It was hard to do nothing, hard not to want to recreate the bonds she'd felt while working with others.

She worked in the park as well, of course. Eco-tourism, introducing people to trees and lemurs, the organisms of an island life; a slow move to economic and environmental stability. The Fish-scale Gecko had colleagues there, a community there, and she enjoyed working with them. What they were doing was valuable; it would provide long-term benefits. But it was all open, lacking entirely in secrecy, and that tore at her, left her shamed.

Do I feel this way because there's more that I could be doing, or because I miss the excitement of it, the danger?

In the end her greatest difficulty was plausibility, because she could almost convince herself that a return to conspiracy had rational support. But that, she knew, was a reasoning supported by ignorance.

The Fish-scale Gecko didn't know how many climate operatives were in Madagascar, if any. She might be the only one. Might be the only one left in the entire region, all of southeast Africa. The numbers changed depending on circumstance and risk, and she knew that the Sand Cat had to keep sourcing more and more people for her network as more of them were compromised.

I might not be able to be as active as I'd like, thought the Fish-scale Gecko, *but maybe I might be able to find someone who can.*

It was a risk. If she were being watched, on the chance she might lead them into caches then she'd be watched if she were meeting someone, as well, and even if that meeting could be explained away for other reasons, the suspicion would only be slightly ameliorated.

So. Communication she couldn't do, perhaps – or not yet. Observation, though . . . a scientist was trained to observe, to record data and analyse. The Fish-scale Gecko knew that was something she excelled at. Not only did it allow her to navigate the forests – and worse, the karst – of the Park, to see the small plants and animals that had otherwise escaped the view of many, but it may have saved her when the realisation that she was being observed herself had dawned.

The suspicion that came upon her – always that feeling of being watched, whether she was out introducing the tourists to forest, or introducing the villagers to tourists – had been too convincing to ignore, and she'd contacted the Stone Wētā, ostensibly for work purposes, and ended the relationship.

So began her silence.

She'd never been able to tell if she had been identified. She suspected not, because there'd been no follow-up, no strange questions or strange people arriving at stranger times, no actionable threat. The watching had been certain, she'd swear to that, and her escape from it a near and thin-worked thing. But it had given her a sense of watchfulness, of what it felt like to be watched. That was a sense she wanted to avoid evoking in others.

If she was going to assess the people she worked with, to discover which of them would be open to conspiracy and willing to sacrifice, she couldn't let them know that she was doing it.

"Did you ever think this would turn out so well, when we started?" she said to one of her co-workers as they waved tourists away, chattering and happy as lemurs as they got onto their bus to be driven back to town. Said it again to the women in the villages, talking to them about their children and their futures – and again to the local officials who helped to smooth the way for new sites, new employment opportunities. "And what do you think we could do better?"

#

Because the fish-scale gecko is restricted to a small region in Madagascar, being primarily found in the limestone karst and nearby deciduous forest of the Ankarana National Park, it is particularly vulnerable to threats. Illegal deforestation, grazing, and mining all endanger its habitat.

#

The Fish-scale Gecko had always been an outdoors person. She didn't much enjoy cities, far preferred the jagged landscape of limestone, the long stretches of forest, to noise and bright lights and the mass press of people, but that preference didn't stop her from visiting the capital on occasion – mostly because her family lived there.

Her young cousin, especially, was a favourite. He was a cheerful little kid, had a real sense of wonder that she enjoyed and wanted to encourage. The Fish-scale Gecko had been invited down for his tenth birthday party and was eager to go. She'd ordered a telescope for him – not expensive, but enough for him to point towards Mars and dream, because the colonisation had been a marvel for him. He followed it along as much as he could, drove his parents crazy with questions they couldn't answer.

"I want to go there one day too," he said, and the Fish-scale Gecko had warned him that he'd have to work hard but she believed he could do it. She didn't speak to him of what he'd leave behind, parents and siblings and her. More important, the forests of his home, the surrounding ocean. She'd have felt as if something were amputated from her if she'd have to leave them, though it was more likely, she admitted to herself, that they'd be taken away. But this was a grief far ahead of him and she couldn't bring herself to squash his enthusiasm. Instead, she'd driven down to Antananarivo, picked up his present, let him open it and dream and smile.

"Do you think I'll be able to see the colony from here?" he said, dancing from foot to foot with excitement as they set it up outside.

"Sorry, but it's not that good a telescope," said the Fish-scale Gecko. "You'll be able to see the Martian ice caps though, according to this." The instruction booklet was spread out in front of them but the light was fading now, and she didn't want to use a torch and get their eyes unaccustomed to the dark.

"You can see the space station from here too, did you know?" said her cousin. "Only for a couple of minutes. It'll be here soon, you don't need a telescope to see it either. I can show you if you like."

"I would, thank you," said the Fish-scale Gecko, and let herself be positioned for best viewing.

"You can see it move," said her cousin. "There, just there! Can you see it?"

"I can see it," she said, squinting. She'd seen it before this, but didn't say, not wanting to begrudge him the ability to share what he'd learned. The space station was brighter than most of the stars in the sky, the sun reflecting off it most visibly close to sunset – and then it shone brighter and brighter, a small starburst of light, and was gone.

"What happened?"

"I don't know," said the Fish-scale Gecko, squinting in the dark and with apprehension rising up, because she'd seen the space station move out of range before and it had never ended like that, and the shock of it, the sudden looseness of her flesh, made her think that perhaps it was because this time, the ending was different.

Her little cousin had his eye pressed to the scope, was swinging it around in wide arcs trying to make himself see, but the Fish-scale Gecko pushed him gently aside, glanced once and then put the lens cap firmly on the telescope and pulled the boy inside to his parents.

"Don't let him look through that thing again tonight," she said.

If they turned on the news they'd soon see why. The Fish-scale

Gecko didn't need the confirmation. She didn't need to ban the child from his toy either – the orbit would take care of the debris – but she needed a few moments alone, to look up and not away, to understand what had just been taken from her. Taken from them all.

The way station to Mars, the place her data would have passed through had it gone, as she'd heard it might, to transport and colonisation. The whispers of a woman in high places. An orbital promise of of exploration, a place to look down from and see the blue planet surviving still for all they did to it.

Gone.

#

The genus that the fish-scale gecko belongs to is notoriously difficult. Differentiating the various species from each other is an ongoing process, as the other members of the genus also have the ability to detach tails and skin – the latter less easily than in the large-scaled fish-scale gecko – and their various colourings can be confusing. Genetic analysis is needed to confirm the true taxonomic status of the genus.

#

The Fish-scale Gecko couldn't look into mirrors now without feeling sick. "I'm so ashamed," she said, over and over, always where no-one could hear because if she explained herself there might be sympathy or understanding and she wanted neither.

She'd been so jealous, her skills and attention put into

abeyance. Had burned with the desire to return to inclusion, even at the risk of others. Had *wanted* the excitement of conspiracy, of collusion and resistance. It had made her feel important. Not just necessary, not just brave, but important. As if what she was doing somehow mattered more, as if that lockbox hidden in the canopy made her superior, somehow, and better than her colleagues. All that wistful recollection, the deliberate smoothing over of the fear she'd sometimes felt in favour of the pride . . . how she'd puffed herself up.

How silly she'd been, how smug.

The explosion of the space station, the loss of all hands, was the first topic of news for a month. Her little cousin was inconsolable; he couldn't understand. "I don't understand either," the Fish-scale Gecko said, hugging him close, and the words burned on her tongue because they were lies, absolute lies, but what more could anyone expect from a woman as sick as she was?

The Fish-scale Gecko knew as soon as she'd seen the explosion, recognised it for what it was, that it had been deliberate.

She didn't say it. She couldn't prove it. And all the debris, the pieces of station, of torn and frozen flesh, were hardly easy for forensics to access. There were explanations of catastrophic failure, but two of those in such a short time . . . the Fish-scale Gecko remembered the failure of a suit, the rescuing of an astronaut by her colleagues, and two such breakdowns didn't speak to her of accident. The whole thing had the shadow of deliberation stamped over it, a warning of threats and the reality of strength and enemy reach.

She no longer wondered if there'd been a climate operative working on that station. She was certain of it now, certain too that the real link between planets had gone, the planet of science cut off from the planet that had come to view science as an obstacle for progress instead of an aid for it. There were already plans to rebuild the station, but they weren't being made by governments, either by themselves or as part of multinational efforts. Instead there were offers from corporations, from the very economic forces that had made the climate network a necessary thing to begin with – that had bought lawmakers and laws and governments, that insulated oligarchs from the genocidal practices of wealth, the apocalyptic consequences of greed and exploitation.

The Fish-scale Gecko trusted none of them.

There was a message waiting for her when she got back to her home. Flowers, a pretty delivery with a card attached, a short message: *I can't ask you to stay.* The card had hearts on it, little kiss marks. Her neighbours teased her when it came, read the card over her shoulder and made noises of protest. "You have to stay! He clearly loves you."

The Fish-scale Gecko blushed appropriately and made her escape, knowing that there was no lover, no romance to be protected. Knowing too that what had come for her wasn't an order, or even a suggestion. It was an acknowledgement of choice, and that she had it.

Stay or go, stay or go. The Japanese Sea Star, so familiar with travel herself, had helped to map a route a long time ago. If she left, slipped out of the skin of her so-public life, she'd lose the protective colouration of her environment, the connections she'd built up around her, the real value of the work she was doing to save the forest. But if she stayed . . .

If she stayed, there might be a real risk of repercussion, and not just for her. When the space station exploded, the Fish-scale Gecko had known in her bones that there was a climate operative aboard. That there'd been six of them seemed overkill. Perhaps the other astronauts had been sympathetic, perhaps not. Perhaps they hadn't even known.

But perhaps . . . perhaps it was hard for those who watched to differentiate between the resistance and those who, however unknowingly, shielded them. The Fish-scale Gecko wasn't the only ardent conservationist in her group. She might not even be the only one under suspicion, and she'd seen in the sky that some targets were spread wide.

THE MARTIAN WĒTĀ

Hemideina maori
In winter, the mountain stone wētā crawls into crevices, into cracks in the stone, and it squats there waiting. It is a creature of summer days and winter strengths, of cryogenic hibernation. When the world freezes around it, becoming a stretch of snow and ice and darkness, the stone wētā freezes solid in its bolthole. Over eighty percent of the water in its body turns to ice. The wētā is climate in a single body. It is a continent broken off, geology made flesh.

When the weather warms, the wētā thaws and resumes its life amidst the stone monuments of the Rock and Pillar range.

#

The Stone Wētā found it harder than she expected to get used to red instead of green, to be so constantly within walls, with a roof hanging over. Sometimes, with the horizon before her, she'd felt more claustrophobic than she had on her colony ship – but that had been a marvel of reduced space, a time of hibernation while she waited for a planet that would take the place of the old.

A data drive still hung between her breasts, but it was there more for symbolism at this point than anything else. All the data she'd brought with her was publicly accessible. "Not that it's much use here," she said, on a planet with an environment so different to the one they'd left that cross-over was minimal. But the climate data was part of a shared heritage that none of the settlers were willing to forego.

The Stone Wētā was not a wilful optimist, and most of her remaining optimism had drained away when news of the space station's destruction arrived. They weren't cut off entirely – information still came through – but the chance of future arrivals had been materially set back. But it was symbolism again, the feeling of an umbilicus broken off, and if there had once been any scientists on Mars who had motivation for destroying data the new distance certainly gave them less incentive to expose themselves.

The Stone Wētā had come to believe that it was easier to be a sleeper agent in winter.

#

Selaginella lepidophylla
A desert dweller, the resurrection plant is adapted to dehydration, to the long dry seasons of its arid environment. When parched for short periods, its outer stems curl into circles, but as the waterless days endure the resurrection plant hunches further down, its inner stems compressing into spirals and minimising surface area. Tucked in, the resurrection

plant survives almost complete desiccation. Until the rains come it takes on the appearance of a dead thing, but beneath the surface there is revival waiting.

#

When the time came to let her interns go, Resurrection took them out into the desert for the final time and opened a bottle of wine to congratulate them. It was a habit of hers to make the final field trip a celebration, something to send her students off into their new lives and make sure they knew she was grateful for the work they'd done.

"It's not really a celebration though, is it?" said Teresa.

"You've done good work," said Resurrection. "You've learned all sorts of new skills. You should be proud."

"I'd be prouder if we got a different result," was the reply. Resurrection had set the pair of them an analysis of change over time, with their own results the final data set. She'd done it for every group she'd had ever since she started working in the protected area.

There was no mistaking the outcome, or the ecological trend. She hadn't expected there to be. The desert of Resurrection's childhood was different in her memory than the desert she saw today. Change in species richness and vegetation cover didn't alter that, and no number of pretty demonstrations with water bottles could distract from what was happening to what was above ground – or what was below it.

"It's not for you to decide the result in advance," she reminded them. "You are scientists. What matters is the evidence. You follow where it takes you and don't falter in it."

Beside her, Verónica drained her wine and said nothing. Resurrection worried for the girl – she'd found evidence of more than science in the desert, and neither of them knew where following it would take her. Resurrection almost wanted to warn her off, but it was no longer enough to train scientists to focus on data alone instead of context. That blindness had cost them all, and dearly.

She had her own glass. Didn't drink more than a sip because she was driving, and that sip was for the toast she made them when she opened the bottle. The rest she poured on the ground when they left, and that ground was empty.

#

The Stone Wētā never copied data now. It would have indicated distrust, and even if she wasn't fully trusting it would have been unwise to bring that distrust to light, an obstacle to the cohesion of community they all needed to survive.

It went against the grain – for so long she'd gone against all her training, kept secrets and pretended to be what she wasn't, but the sight of the wētā draped over her flesh with its inked and spindly legs, and the comforting weight of breasts, no longer new but a normal part of the body she'd always wanted, reminded her that pretending had never gone well for her before.

She'd never been able to pretend her way into masculinity, never been able to pretend that what was happening to the data of her colleagues was a minor thing.

So she told them, all of them, who she was. She'd never made a secret of it on the voyage, and had spoken plainly to the few who'd guessed and asked, but she hadn't advertised it. Then the station orbiting Earth blew up, taking with it a woman who'd helped her on the way, and the Stone Wētā had called a meeting.

"This is what I am," she said. "This is what I've done. This is what I've brought."

They were all scientists together, and she couldn't afford to treat them as less.

#

Scolymastra joubini
The glass sponge crouches on sea beds beneath the Antarctic ice. The silica skeleton sways in the dark water, chilled by the currents of a continent. It is the oldest organism on the planet; for 15,000 years, perhaps, the glass sponge has endured a long night, its growth a slow and silent thing. But the ice shelves collapsing above have brought light and plankton in levels the glass sponge is not accustomed to. It grows wildly, branching out quickly, while destruction takes place above it.

#

The Glass Sponge had learned habit from destruction. Learned, too, that her own reflection in ice was a terrible thing.

"Am I a complete coward?" she asked. "I've gone on so long, in the dark, expecting it all to be the same." And then she'd let a friend be taken in her place, the secrecy and necessity of her under-life become a priority above all others, and the destruction caused by that choice had brought her behaviour into light, given her endless opportunity to reassess her actions. "I lie awake at night and wonder what I should have done differently," she said, all her certainty melting like the ice she'd spent so much of her life on.

"The bargains I have made," she said. "The friendships gone, the loss of respect – from her peers and from herself.

"The bargains *we* made," said Dave. "At least your motive was good." The protection of climate, and of science, compared to the protection of adultery. He loved his wife, the Glass Sponge knew, but what marriage wouldn't crumble under the weight of such a secret?

She couldn't think of her own naiveté without cringing. All the idealism she'd had, all the actions she'd debated. The ability of her own government to resist, the comparison with the national history of nuclear activism. It had all been so optimistic.

She didn't even know where her friend had gone. Scott Base was New Zealand jurisdiction, but just after landing in Christchurch Lexi had disappeared from a holding cell, and the Glass Sponge didn't believe it was coincidence.

"She could have escaped," she said, aware as she said it that it was a lame explanation. Either their own government was in on it, or Lexi had disappeared because they weren't.

"I can't live like this anymore," she said, her dreams full of absence and rainbow boats, of melting ice caps and mushroom clouds and sinking into deep water. "I want to believe that we can be more than this."

The day she got off the ice she flew to Wellington, and the next morning the Glass Sponge dressed with grim care, as if for exposure. She marched herself past the Parliament buildings and into Environment House, home to the Members of Parliament responsible for the environment and for climate change. She had with her the most responsible journalist she knew. "I need to speak to the Ministers," she said.

#

Felis margarita
The sand cat protects itself from sunlight, and from the lack of it. The desert is a place of extreme temperatures and the bottom of the sand cat's feet, the spaces between its toes, are thick with fur for when the sand is scalding in the noon sun. This fur blurs its footsteps, and the tracks of the sand cat through the dunes are hard to follow.

The sand cat, relative to its size, bites harder than any other feline.

#

The advantage to having a local network as well as an international one was breadth and immediacy. The Sand Cat had been preparing dinner when she realised she was out of onions, and was making a quick run to market when her neighbour caught up with her.

"Two strange men drove up to your house," she said. "They knocked on the door and went straight in." She'd seen the Sand Cat set off minutes before, and knew her husband was working late at the hospital that month, and her uncle down in Bamako visiting relations. "They left their car outside the door." She shook her head. "Something's not right. I'd say come home with me, but . . ." But she was next door, and easy to notice. "Do you have somewhere to go?" she said. "Can I call anyone for you?"

"It's probably just a couple of friends of my husband," said the Sand Cat, knowing full well that it wasn't. "I'll give him a call. Thank you for letting me know," she said. "But you should go home now. You haven't seen me, understand?"

She called her husband as the other woman hurried off. "I'm just getting some meat for dinner," she said, naming a butcher's shop that was twenty minutes out of her way, and in the other direction. "Would you prefer chicken or goat?" It was a question they'd thought up together, perfectly innocuous, perfectly unnoticeable.

"Goat, please," he said. "And will you make that special bread you do, you know, your mother's recipe?"

(*I understand*, he didn't say. *I'm not alone. Be careful.*)

"Of course I will," she said, and it was an effort to make her voice as cheerful as it should have been. "I'll see you soon. I love you."

The Sand Cat dropped her mobile into the nearest rubbish bin, careful to keep her head down and to avoid attention as she walked to the city outskirts, leaving her life behind and going into the desert. The sun was going down, and darkness covered her.

#

Geckolepis megalepis
The fish-scale gecko is an escape artist of particular and gruesome aspect. Its sister-species amputate themselves in the face of predation, but the fish-scale gecko holds its escape in its skin instead of its tail. That skin is large-plated and scaly, and its attachment to the flesh beneath is temporary. When the fish-scale gecko is grabbed or threatened, it sheds its skin and skitters, bald and pulsing, into the trees.

#

The woman gave the Fish-scale Gecko an extra blanket, and a cup of tea to take away the chill. She was still shaking – as well as she knew the forest, it was a different place at night and she hadn't wanted to risk much light. It was lucky the moon was out, lucky she knew ropes and climbing enough to do it blindfolded, if necessary.

She'd kept a pack hidden in a distant canopy, stuffed with false papers and basic supplies. Something she'd arranged after the first data drop, when the possible need for escape had been so strongly on her mind, and the identification with arboreal creatures an ever-present one. She took the data box too, rescued it from a second site, the skin scraped from her body as she clambered up through branches.

Her host she knew less well than she'd have liked. A nurse from one of the outlying villages, a widow who'd shown interest at village meetings, when the Fish-scale Gecko had come to give talks on the economic benefits of eco-tourism. There was a first aid kit in her pack but she'd fallen into karst, trying to skirt enough for secrecy, and the laceration down one leg required stitches.

"Please don't say anything," she begged. "I can't go to a hospital."

"It's not my business to give my patients away," said the nurse. She worked quickly, careful and clean, doing what she could to hold the skin together. "I ask no questions. But there is someone I know who works with women sometimes, if their husbands or family are unkind. She keeps them secret and helps them move."

It was craven, perhaps, taking on the character of a battered woman. But it was camouflage as well, and the Fish-scale Gecko had worked and lied and bled for the data she had with her and she could not endanger it now.

"Thank you," she said, swallowing her pride. "I need the help."

#

"I miss him."

The Stone Wētā waited, knowing there was nothing to be said to make it better. The colonists had left a lot behind, friends and family the most and least of it, but they'd left, most of them, confidently. Believing the people they'd left were safe and happy.

They'd been interested in space travel, all of them. Wouldn't have come to a new planet if they weren't, and wouldn't have then made friends with others who shared that interest, who'd become astronauts instead of colonists. Who'd died with their own colleagues, orbiting the planet they'd never entirely chosen to leave.

"And you think it's because of this. Because of this climate data."

"Yes," said the Stone Wētā. She'd had this same conversation a number of times – with people who'd known the dead astronauts well, from people who'd only had passing conversations with them on their way up but were disturbed nevertheless. From people, even, who'd never met any of them, but who had scientist friends left on Earth.

"I see." The clenched jaw, the clenched fists. The Stone Wētā had seen these things before. "This is not the news I ever wanted," she heard.

It hurt her that none of them truly seemed surprised. *What did we give up when we came here*, she thought. *What did I give up?*

#

Asterias amurensis
The Japanese sea star owes its success to adaptability and reproductive strategy. It owes that success, as well, to the interconnection of the world. Its larvae, spread through ballast waters, are shipped to other oceans and other countries. It is one of the most invasive species alive, and there is hungry persistence in each of its five arms.

#

They caught her at port, waiting for an international ferry. "I suppose even the stupidest, most irresponsible merchant seaman checks his bilge water occasionally," she said. There was no point trying to deny anything, no point to calling for legal assistance. They had her handbag, were rooting through it with all the elegance of oafs, and to tell them she was coming back from a conference was a limited truth at best.

The drives at least were anonymous. Some she'd been able to disperse, and these were the minority – new research being passed on to her so that she could make copies again and distribute them. Some of that research had already been published, in reduced form, and a simple comparison would be enough to blow her identity. Since the destruction of the space station, the Japanese Sea Star had begun to wonder if her level of relative fame would be any protection after all. *Clearly a delusion*, she thought, with a brief grim amusement. *A confusion of colour and clarity.*

Colour, in the natural world, gained attention and respect. It also signified toxin. A difficult balancing act, and one she'd failed to judge sufficiently.

"I'm sorry it's come to this," said her interrogator. "Really, I am. We would have preferred to work with you. There's no profit to us in doing it the hard way – and none to you either."

"We both have very different understandings of the word profit," said the Japanese Sea Star. She smiled at him, polite and humourless. "I suspect mine is the less pedestrian."

Her interrogator smiled back, equally humourless. His dimples were plastic things, entirely artificial. "You think you're so smart," he said. "So above the rest of us. Look where you're sitting, lady. What has smart got you?"

"Self-respect," said the Japanese Sea Star.

#

"We've held ourselves apart too long."

The Stone Wētā, in another life, had thought it was her influence that took a previously untried individual and exposed her to the possibilities of a new life. But the Martian colony was not an individual. It was a community – one that argued and fought and tested to breaking – and it was beyond her small influence.

"We're scientists. For too long we've told ourselves that that's all we are. It's not enough anymore. We can't stand by and do nothing. We can't recognise what's happening and stay silent. People will say it's easy for us to speak up now, when there's nothing to lose. That is a lie."

The Stone Wētā listened with the rest, and nodded. There was a certain freedom of speech on the colony, one that would no doubt have its own future challenges. But outsiders had little influence here, and while the destruction of the space station might have caused colony collapse, they set themselves tight restrictions and aimed for sustainability. There was no guarantee, with what they were about to do, that any help would come from Earth again.

"We might be starved, we might be damaged. We might die. Perhaps that's the price of speech. Perhaps it's what we've earned by staying silent. But it's not going to stop us doing better."

The colony had solar panels, the ability to transmit information to Earth. Any information, as much as they wanted. As long as they wanted.

The Stone Wētā felt a tap on her shoulder. It was the head

of the botanical department, who was looking to establish lichens like *Buellia* over the surface of Mars, an early stage of terraforming.

"Not that I object," he said, "but does it strike you at all as hypocritical that we're protesting the deliberate change of climate on one planet at the same time as we're trying to change the climate on this one?"

"Believe me, mate," said the Stone Wētā, laughing, "it really bloody does."

#

Dendrocnide moroides
The gympie gympie covers itself with stinging hairs and neurotoxin. It is one of the most poisonous plants in the world, and one of the most painful. A human who brushes up against a gympie gympie will experience agony for up to two years: a persistent reminder of trespass.

It flourishes best after disturbance, when the ground is overturned and in full sunlight.

#

When the Gympie Gympie was a little girl she'd heard the stories from her grandmother, who had heard them from *her* grandmother, about a long slow war that cut all of her people down around her.

She wanted to say, grown now and with her grandmother dead, with all her grandmothers dead, that she never expected such a war to happen again in her lifetime. Wanted to say it, but never could. It hadn't escaped her that disturbance had become ubiquitous, and that ubiquity was nonetheless focused on communities that didn't have the weapons for fighting back, or not the weapons that had come to count.

The Gympie Gympie had seen what had happened to her own lands. Seen what had happened to the lands of other peoples in other countries, seen where the burden of managing the change had fallen. The patterns were all too familiar.

She'd been expecting war for quite some time, and when the first transmissions from Mars began to arrive on Earth, she realised that, for all its opening skirmishes, the war for climate had finally started.

#

Pinus longaeva
The bristlecone pine of the American south-west grows slowly, perhaps increasing its diameter as little as several centimetres per century, but it does grow. The tree is so accustomed to cold and aridity that it can colonise mountain tops where few other trees can grow, and it is so long-lived in these environments that a bristlecone pine planted today might still be alive when humans have colonised other star systems.

#

"Persistence," said the Bristlecone Pine, "is what differentiates adaptation." It was an archaeological class that she spoke to, not students who were typically and primarily concerned with climate change and ecology, but she trusted that they could draw the parallels.

"This isn't an extraordinary phenomenon," she said. "It's plain common sense. If a new type of pot is more useful than the old – maybe it holds more, or is waterproof, or is easier to make – then it will become increasingly more present in the record than a pot that's less useful, or falls to pieces not long after use." She pointed to a boy in the first row, who'd made a particularly terrible attempt at clay-work in a recent workshop on ancient technique. "I know you know what I'm talking about.

"The same is true," she continued, "of information. Useful information gets passed on – in records, in teaching. In stories. It's how we know which snakes to avoid, what plants to eat. The more widespread that useful information is, the greater the opportunity it has to survive. You'll note that none of you are currently suffering from smallpox, due to the spread of information about vaccines. But sometimes, and we see this, for example, in some rituals or customs, information is restricted to certain groups. Can anyone tell me why, or give an example?"

She knew damn well what the first example offered would be.

"An example that's related to archaeology, and not the Martian situation?" About half the hands went down, which was disappointing, but Bristlecone Pine couldn't risk the appearance of bias. She did not want to end up like her predecessor, and if data that couldn't be shared was always at risk, then there was data, too, that was dangerous in itself.

#

The Fish-eating Spider stared up into the dark. She missed the waters of her own country, but she could no longer say what country it was that held those waters – the old home, or the new. It was harder to miss the earth of either; the way it smelled when she turned it over for burial. That was homesickness turned into plain sickness, the guilt of regret and necessity both.

Those countries, both of them, were behind her now, here in this place where even the stars were different, the Southern Cross nowhere in sight. She knocked again, and when the door opened she saw a girl her own age, with familiar eyes.

I'm not a soldier, she thought. *I don't know what I am. But if I have to fight, I'll do it my way.*

"I'm sorry to bother you," she said. "But I think I knew your father."

Resistance might be preservation, and it might be survival, but if it were honest it was also price, and consequence.

ABOUT THE AUTHOR

Octavia Cade is a New Zealand writer with a PhD in science communication. She's had over 40 short stories published in markets such as *Clarkesworld*, *Asimov's*, and *Shimmer*, as well as several novellas, two poetry collections, and a collection of nonfiction essays.

Octavia has won three Sir Julius Vogel awards, attended Clarion West 2016, and is the 2020 Massey University / SquareEdge writer in residence.

ALSO FROM PAPER ROAD PRESS

NO MAN'S LAND
A.J. FITZWATER

Dorothea 'Tea' Gray joins the Land Service and is sent to work on a remote farm, one of many young women left to fill the empty shoes left by fathers and brothers serving in the Second World War.

But Tea finds more than hard work and hot sun in the dusty North Otago nowhere – she finds a magic inside herself she never could have imagined, a way to save her brother in a distant land she never thought she could reach, and a love she never knew existed.

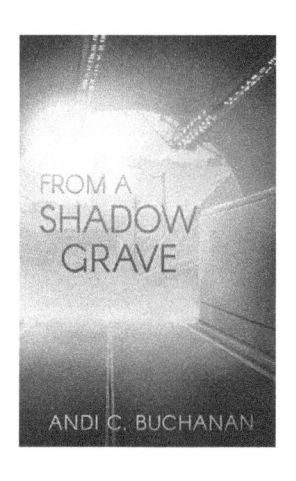

FROM A SHADOW GRAVE
ANDI C. BUCHANAN

Wellington, 1931. Seventeen-year-old Phyllis Symons's body is discovered in the Mount Victoria tunnel construction site.

Eighty years later, Aroha Brooke is determined to save her life.

"Haunting in every sense of the word" – Charles Payseur, Quick Sip Reviews

AT THE EDGE
EDITED BY DAN RABARTS AND LEE MURRAY

From the brink of civilisation, the fringe of reason, and the border of reality, come 22 stories infused with the bloody-minded spirit of the Antipodes.

Winner of the Sir Julius Vogel Award for Best Collected Work, 2017

"Lovecraftian horrors to please the most cosmic of palates" – Angela Slatter

SHORTCUTS: TRACK 1
EDITED BY MARIE HODGKINSON

Strange tales of Aotearoa New Zealand. Seven Kiwi authors weave stories of people and creatures displaced in time and space, risky odysseys, and dangerous discoveries.

Winner of the Sir Julius Vogel Award for Best Novella: Octavia Cade, *The Ghost of Matter*

"Six of the best" – Phillip Mann

BABY TEETH: BITE-SIZED TALES OF TERROR
EDITED BY DAN RABARTS AND LEE MURRAY

Kids say the creepiest things. Twenty-seven stories about the strange, unexpected, and downright terrifying sides of parenthood.

Leave the lights on tonight. So you'll see them coming.

Winner of the Sir Julius Vogel Award for Best Collected Work, 2014

Winner of the Australian Shadows Award for Edited Publication, 2014

CPSIA information can be obtained
at www.ICGtesting.com
Printed in the USA
LVHW091937160921
697980LV00007BE/1175